Sir Philip's Folly

Sir Philip's Folly

M. C. BEATON

BLACK
STONE
PUBLISHING

Copyright © 1993 by Marion Chesney
Published in 2018 by Blackstone Publishing
Cover and book design by Blackstone Publishing

Printed in the United States of America

ISBN 978-1-9825-2564-4
Fiction / Romance / Regency

1 3 5 7 9 10 8 6 4 2

CIP data for this book is available
from the Library of Congress

Blackstone Publishing
31 Mistletoe Rd.
Ashland, OR 97520

www.BlackstonePublishing.com

For Ann Robinson and her daughter,
Emma Wilson, with love.

CHAPTER ONE

*T*he atmosphere in the Poor Relation in Bond Street was glacial. It was as if the owners meant to banish the vulgar air emanating from Mrs. Mary Budge by producing an aristocratic frost—the owners with the exception of Sir Philip Sommerville, who had been instrumental in introducing Mrs. Budge to the hotel.

Even the servants found Mrs. Budge gross and vulgar. She was fat, not cosy armfuls of fat, but solid, rather threatening fat, with two huge bosoms like stuffed cushions pushed up under her many chins. Although lodged in the sitting-room of the apartment next door to the hotel, which the owners used as their living quarters, she went on like a guest, demanding meals to be served to her at all hours of the day.

The hotel had been founded a few years before by Lady Amelia Fortescue, whose former home it was; Lady Fortescue, tall, white-haired and still upright and elegant in her seventies. At her right hand was Colonel Sandhurst, an equally handsome seventyish with silver hair and childlike blue eyes. Also an owner was Miss Tonks, spinster, still slightly faded-looking and inclined, now she was in her forties, to mourn in private over the state of marriage that never was, but her sheeplike face carried a certain newfound air of authority. Her descent into trade had benefited her character. There had been six of them at the start. Now there were four, and four who might have been happy had not Sir Philip fallen in love with the quite dreadful Mrs. Budge and brought her home to roost.

The other three, that is Lady Fortescue, Colonel Sandhurst and Miss Tonks, held a council of war one afternoon when Sir Philip was out driving with his lady-love. The thing that hurt Miss Tonks most of all was that the elderly Sir Philip, before the advent of Mrs. Budge, had seemed to be becoming affectionate towards *her*. Added to that, Sir Philip had cleaned himself up for the horrible Mrs. Budge the way he had not bothered to do for her. The improved fortunes of the former poor relations who ran the hotel meant that they had money to dress well, and Sir Philip, albeit still like an elderly tortoise, looked, well, almost a gentleman in a new swallow-tail coat of Weston's tailoring and sporting a nut-brown wig which actually looked real.

Lady Fortescue was also feeling piqued, although she would not admit it to herself. For Sir Philip, before he had gone off to Warwick for the wedding of one of the former owners, had shown every evidence of being enamoured with *her*. Only Colonel Sandhurst simply wanted Mrs. Budge out because she was vulgar and offensive and, as he said, with a little flick of his new silver snuff-box, "Common as a barber's chair and bad for trade."

What if the Prince Regent, who had recently honoured them with a visit to their now famous dining-room, should decide to return? Mrs. Budge had been banned from the dining-room, but on a couple of occasions had coerced Sir Philip into squiring her there for a meal. Lady Fortescue and Colonel Sandhurst, who made a show of waiting table, part of the cachet of the hotel being that the guests were served by aristocrats, had refused to serve her on the last occasion, which had resulted in a waspish scene with Sir Philip.

The three owners were in the small office at the back of the entrance hall.

"I am sure it is Mrs. Budge who is beginning to turn away customers," said Lady Fortescue. "The Rochesters and Bensonhursts have cancelled. I know it is not the Season, but we had hoped to be booked up all year round, and now this. Two of our best apartments lying empty!"

The colonel longed to say there was an easy way out of all this. He and Lady Fortescue should marry, sell the hotel and retire to the country. He had thought Lady Fortescue had been going to agree to this plan, and only a few weeks ago, but the Prince Regent had come to dine, and Lady Fortescue had promptly forgotten all plans of marriage.

Instead he said, "Sir Philip will tire of her soon. He has always been generous with other people's money. He will become tired of her leeching on him."

"But the expense of that dreadful woman is being borne by all of us," said Miss Tonks.

"Then, as a first move," said Lady Fortescue, "we will take a careful account of everything that Mrs. Budge costs us, including her share of rent, and we will deduct the bill from Sir Philip's share of the proceeds."

A flash of rare malice shone in the colonel's eyes. "That should fix him."

"How could he?" asked Miss Tonks, not for the first time. "Her very presence humiliates us all."

"He is grown silly in his old age," said Lady Fortescue.

"He went off in a rage because for some reason he thought we should have told him about the Prince Regent's visit, but how were we to get word to him? I gather that you, Miss Tonks, and Sir Philip broke your journey from Warwickshire at some inn in Chipping Norton. How were we to know that? But he stamped out and that was when Mrs. Budge found him, in Hyde Park, and took him home to that squalid flat she has in a mews, a flat which she promptly let before moving in with us."

"There is another, graver, problem," said the colonel. "We have all been guilty of theft in order to finance this hotel, either by direct action or by association. If Sir Philip ever tells his lady that, then even if he tires of her, she is in a position to blackmail us into letting her stay. Worse, she could go to the authorities and we would all end up swinging on the end of a rope outside Newgate."

"A pox on the silly old fool," raged Lady Fortescue. "How can we stop him?"

"I told him the other day if he ever breathed a word of what we had been up to I would shoot him," said the colonel. "I think he believed me, but I am not sure. He is so besotted, he does not seem to realize that it is his neck he has to worry about as well. But I will tell him on his return about Mrs. Budge's bills."

"No, I think I would like to do that," said Lady Fortescue. She looked up as the hotel footman appeared in the doorway. "What is it, Jack?"

"There is a Lady Carruthers has called and is desirous to speak to you, my lady."

Lady Fortescue rose to her feet. "Put her in the coffee room and Colonel Sandhurst and I will be with her directly. Your arm, Colonel."

Miss Tonks bit her lip. Everything had changed. Her

friend and former partner, Mrs. Budley, was now married and on her honeymoon, Sir Philip was crawling around after that dreadful woman, and the colonel and Lady Fortescue often went on as if she, Miss Tonks, were one of the hotel servants instead of a partner.

Lady Fortescue and Colonel Sandhurst, the one as tall and erect as the other despite their advanced years, made their stately way to the coffee room. A lady dressed in the height of fashion was sitting on a chair by the window, her maid standing to one side, and a footman at the other end of the room holding her pug-dog.

Lady Carruthers was as highly painted as a trollop, but that was not unusual in this age of transparent dresses and rouged faces. She had perhaps been a beauty at one time, but discontent had given her thin mouth a petulant droop, and social hauteur her eyes a steely look. Her bonnet was as feathered as any Indian's head-dress and her silk pelisse was edged with ermine. She did not rise at the approach of Lady Fortescue and Colonel Sandhurst, contenting herself with a small inclination of her head which made the feathers in her bonnet dance and quiver.

Lady Fortescue did not curtsy but inclined her own head and raised her thin black eyebrows. "Lady Carruthers?"

Lady Carruthers nodded again. Lady Fortescue sat down opposite her, with the colonel standing behind her chair.

"How may we help you?"

Trying to remind herself that these were mere hoteliers, Lady Carruthers was nonetheless impressed.

"The roof of my town house fell in last night," she began. "I am desirous of finding accommodation until the repairs have been effected."

"We have a fine apartment by chance," said Lady Fortescue. "Will Lord Carruthers be joining you?"

"My husband is dead. I am very young to be a widow, I know."

Lady Fortescue judged Lady Carruthers to be nearly forty. "My daughter is with me," went on Lady Carruthers. "My little Arabella. Such a dear child and such a comfort to me. My maid will need a room, and also I must have at least one footman."

"There is accommodation for your servants."

Lady Fortescue opened her reticule and took out a gilt-edged card which she laid on the table in front of Lady Carruthers. "Our terms," she murmured.

Lady Carruthers fumbled in her bosom for her quizzing -glass. She looked at the prices and her eyes widened. But a hotel patronized by the Prince Regent himself naturally would have high rates. Affecting indifference, she pushed the card away. "Quite," she said. "It would suit me to move in today."

"Our pleasure." Lady Fortescue inclined her head again and the colonel gave a little bow from the waist.

"Hotel life might amuse my little Arabella." Lady Fortescue got to her feet. "And it is hard to amuse schoolroom misses these days."

***

Miss Arabella Carruthers stood at the window of the drawing-room and looked idly down into the street. She was not often allowed in the drawing-room of the town house, being mostly confined to the schoolroom, which was on the top floor. But the roof had fallen in and the schoolroom was no more.

Although she was nineteen years old, Arabella looked considerably younger. Her mother liked to pretend her daughter was a mere schoolchild, and so Arabella wore smocked dresses and her long brown hair down her back. She enlivened the tedium of her days by reading a great deal. She was not encouraged to have friends; any friends of her own age might damage the fiction that she was considerably younger than nineteen.

She had accepted this state of affairs, not really having any other way of life to set against it. She had lived in the country until the death of her father the previous year. Her mother and father had never at any time seemed very close, each going their separate ways, her father immersed in sport, her mother in competing with other landowners' wives for social ascendency. Arabella had progressed tranquilly from nursemaid to governess, living, apart from the company of servants, a fairly isolated life.

She looked idly down into the street below, not aware that her life was about to change dramatically and that this change was to start with falling in love. As she watched the carriages come and go in the fashionable square, she noticed a very smart phaeton driven by a tall gentleman rounding the square. It came to a stop at the house next door. The driver called to his tiger to go to the horses's heads and then jumped down. A lady and her maid came along the pavement. He swept off his hat and stood talking to them.

The sunlight glinted on his golden hair. He was wearing a long biscuit-coloured coat of superb cut with many capes. The lady and her maid moved on. He turned to enter the house next door and then, as if aware of the steady gaze looking down on him, he stared up, full at Arabella.

His face was lightly tanned, his eyes very blue. He suddenly smiled and raised the curly brimmed beaver he was holding in his hand in salute. And then he went on indoors.

Arabella stood transfixed. He was the man of her dreams. She turned and ran from the room and down to the hall, where one of the footmen was lounging on a bench.

"Who lives next door?" she asked.

He stood up. "Old Lady Marchant, miss."

"No one else?"

"Her companion, a Miss Tipps, I believe, also elderly."

"Oh, but a very grand and handsome man has just called. His carriage is outside."

The footman smiled on her indulgently. "You just wait there, miss, and I'll go and ask his servant."

He was back in a few minutes. "The gentleman you saw, Miss Arabella, is the Earl of Denby."

"And he does not live in this square?"

"Not this square, no. Berkeley Square."

"Thank you, John."

Arabella went slowly up the stairs. Now, if she were to have a proper Season as befitted her age, she would have a chance of meeting him. Perhaps he was married! But at least she had someone to dream about and that was one small comfort. But whether she would even get a chance to see him again was surely highly unlikely.

***

Sir Philip that evening looked down wrathfully at the bill Lady Fortescue had just presented to him. "This is outrageous," he spluttered.

Lady Fortescue's voice dripped ice. "We are hardworking hoteliers and cannot afford such luxuries as supporting the greedy indulgences of your paramour. There is not only her rent there, but her dressmaker's bills, her mantua-maker's demands, not to mention those of perfumer and milliner, and so on."

"But I have yet to pay Weston!"

"Then you must economize. We were fortunate in letting one suite to Lady Carruthers today. But the other best one lies vacant. You know our guests are at best notoriously slow at paying their bills. Neither myself nor the colonel nor Miss Tonks wants Mrs. Budge here. She lowers the tone of the place."

"I will not listen to any criticism of my Mary."

"*Your* Mary. Unless you get rid of that female, I shall sell this hotel from under her!"

"You cannot!"

"It is still my house."

"But we are partners!"

"The majority decision will hold. Miss Tonks is distressed and the colonel wants me to sell anyway. Perhaps while I am making up my mind exactly what to do, you can begin to attend to your duties here as before. It is time you waited in the dining-room again and gave the colonel an evening off."

"Is this all the gratitude I get?" howled Sir Philip. "Who raised the wind to get this place started? Who stole–?" He broke off in confusion. He had stolen a valuable necklace from the Duke of Rowcester and replaced it with a clever copy. He had not told any of the other poor relations what he had taken. The jeweller he had sold the necklace to still had it in keeping, and Sir Philip was paying him a weekly sum to do so in the hope that one day he could buy it back and replace it. For sooner or later the duke was going to take that necklace out of its glass case in the muniments room to show someone, and that someone might be sharp enough to recognize a fake.

"Stole what?" demanded Lady Fortescue sharply.

"Never mind," muttered Sir Philip. He glanced up at her. He still felt a tug at his heart when he looked at her and a desire to please her. He picked up the bill. "If I can find someone to take the other apartment, may I delay payment of this until after I have settled my tailor's bill?"

"Very well." Lady Fortescue grasped the silver knob of her stick and leaned forward, her black eyes suddenly kind.

"I can understand a man of your years being easily prey to infatuation, Sir Philip. But try to stand back a little and survey Mrs. Budge as she really is."

He stood up. "Mrs. Budge is warm and affectionate, ma'am. She cares for me. I have been alone too long. I am ... I am thinking of marrying her."

"If you do, then you must definitely leave the hotel or we must sell," said Lady Fortescue quietly.

When Sir Philip had left, Lady Fortescue sat and thought briefly about poisoning Mary Budge. She could only hope that Sir Philip would come to his senses.

Miss Tonks walked into the office, looking flustered and nervous.

"Miss Tonks, what can we do for you?" asked Lady Fortescue. She automatically used "we," not like royalty, but because she was so used to having the colonel next to her.

"I wish to ask Monsieur André to arrange my hair."

Monsieur André was the court hairdresser.

Lady Fortescue looked surprised. "The decision is yours, Miss Tonks. The colonel showed you how to open an account at the bank some time ago and I believe you to be thrifty. If you wish to spend your money on such luxuries, it is your decision. But why? We have no important social engagements, although"–she gave a sigh–"the only social engagements we have these days is when we are asked to cater at some house."

"I felt like doing something," said Miss Tonks, looking flustered.

"I know you had a sad adventure where you shot that highwayman on the road to Warwickshire," said Lady Fortescue. "But did something else happen? You have not been yourself since your return, Miss Tonks."

Miss Tonks thought briefly of the journey back with Sir Philip when they had been friends and when she had hoped that they might marry and that at last she would have the right to put the magic title of "Mrs." before her name. But she said, "I am a little tired, that is all. Did you present Sir Philip with his bill?"

"Yes, but I cannot seem to change his mind about Mrs. Budge. Dreadful woman. She eats like a horse. And her language? I swear she is related to half the costermongers in London. I wonder if Sir Philip is telling her to economize. That should be interesting."

* * *

Sir Philip was trying to do just that. Mrs. Budge was sitting before the fire in the sitting-room of the apartment which the poor relations rented. A table was spread with an assortment of pies and jellies and bottles of wine. Sir Philip, who enjoyed his love's Falstaffian appetite, nonetheless shuddered at the thought of the cost.

"But, my heart," said Mrs. Budge between mouthfuls, "you told me this was *your* hotel."

"Well, it is, but in partnership."

"So who are the others?"

"Why, Lady Fortescue, Colonel Sandhurst and Miss Tonks."

"But that's only four of you, and you must be coining money in a place like this."

He took one of her plump hands in his despite the fact that it was holding a fork. "It costs a lot to keep a place like this going," he pleaded. "You know what society's like. Never pay their bills."

"So why bother about paying yours?"

"Because they are my friends."

"Fine friends they've turned out to be."

"Now, my heart, I won't let them criticize you, but I also won't let you criticize them."

She leaned forward and gave him a smacking kiss on the mouth which tasted of apple pie from the crumbs on her lips. "You worry too much," she said softly. "It's just as well you've got me to look after you."

He smiled at her weakly and placed one of his small, white, well-cared-for manicured hands on one of her enormous breasts. She playfully slapped his hand away. "Let me eat first," she said.

He got to his feet. "Where are you going?" she asked.

"I'm going to see if I can find a client to take the missing rooms. Limmer's often has a few dissatisfied guests. I'll go there."

"Wait until I finish eating and I'll come with you."

"Limmer's is not the place for ladies. I will not be long."

After he had gone, Mrs. Budge ate everything in sight. Betty and John, Lady Fortescue's old servants, were supposed to wait on the poor relations, but Mrs. Budge knew from experience that if she rang the bell they would refuse to answer. Marriage was the solution. But perhaps first she should see if she could get Sir Philip to buy her some jewelry. Jewelry was better than money in the bank any day.

***

Lady Fortescue and Miss Tonks showed Lady Carruthers and Arabella to their new quarters. "Don't let any of these hotel servants put on airs," Arabella's mother had told her. "They may be of good background, but now they are in trade, and don't you forget it." So Arabella was amused to see that Lady Fortescue's grand manner was reducing her mother to something approaching civility.

"We will dine in our sitting-room this evening," said Lady Carruthers.

"Dinner for all is served in the dining-room, Lady Carruthers."

"Am I to eat in a common dining-room?"

"The Prince Regent was not too high in the instep to do so." Lady Fortescue moved to the door. "Dinner is at eight."

"Eight!" exclaimed Arabella after she had gone. "Dinner in the country is at four."

"You must get used to London ways."

"Talking about getting used to London ways, Mama, I have been meaning to ask you: When am I making my come-out?"

"My dear child, you are too young!"

"I am all of nineteen."

Lady Carruthers winced and then said with an affected vagueness. "You surprise me."

"But it is true, and I am still in these dreadful frocks and with my hair down."

Arabella privately thought her mother's wardrobe of jeune fille gowns should be altered to fit herself while her mother dressed her age.

"The point is," said Lady Carruthers, "that it is hard to remember your age when I look so young. I am used to the state of marriage and do not like being a widow. That is why we are come to London."

"I do not understand you, Mama."

Her mother gave a well-practised trill of laughter. "Why, it is my come-out. I cannot appear at the Season like a débutante. So much more discreet to come to London now. There are plenty of eligible men around."

Arabella thought of the handsome man she had seen

with a sort of despair. She would never get out in society. Mama would fail and they would return to the country for the long winter and then back to Town for Mama to try again while she, Arabella, grew older and dowdier and the earl married someone else. Of course, he might be married already. She almost hoped he were then she would not have to think about him every minute, which is what she had been doing since she had seen him.

She missed having friends. It would be wonderful to have a friend to confide in, to talk to about the earl, to share her dreams.

She thought wearily that she would probably never see the earl again.

***

Sir Philip made his way into Limmer's coffee room. It was thin of company but he took a table, ordered a bottle of wine and looked about him with his sharp old eyes. Limmer's catered for the sporting fraternity, and there were two Corinthians slouched at one table. One of them had his muddy boots up on the seat opposite and the other had his teeth filed to a point so that he could spit through them like a coachman. There were three men in the livery of the Four-in-Hand Club at another table, talking horseflesh in loud, drawling voices. Sir Philip knew them all. Not much hope there, he thought.

And then a tall man walked in and stood in the centre of the room, looking about him with an easy air of authority. His golden hair curled under the rim of his curly-brimmed beaver, which he had not removed, showing he did not plan to stay in the coffee room above ten minutes, as did the stick and gloves he held in one white hand. His face was classically handsome. Sir Philip judged him to be in his early thirties. He summoned the waiter and asked in an urgent whisper who the newcomer was.

"The Earl of Denby," whispered the waiter. "Resident here."

Sir Philip rose to his feet, bared his china teeth in an ingratiating smile, and said, "Lord Denby! What a pleasure to see you, my lord."

The earl looked in surprise at the old gentleman who was leering at him. Must be some friend of mother's, he thought. He crossed to Sir Philip's table.

"Your servant, sir," he said. "But I have a poor memory and you have the advantage of me."

"Sir Philip Sommerville, at your service. Pray join me in a glass of wine."

The earl sat down reluctantly.

"When did we meet?" he asked. "Was it at my mother's?"

"Ah, that would be it," said Sir Philip mendaciously. "I am surprised to see you in a hotel such as this, my lord. Town house being repaired?"

"My mother is in residence there. I mostly spend my days in the country, and so I see no reason to disrupt her household by joining her. But you have a point. This hotel is none too clean."

"I am part owner of the Poor Relation," said Sir Philip.

The earl's handsome face stiffened slightly. "And no doubt you are about to tell me I would be better there?"

"Why not?" demanded Sir Philip with a cheek that the earl found himself admiring. "The food's the talk of London, the sheets are clean, the rooms well-appointed. You are about to freeze up and say, 'How dare you tout your wares?' but I am a businessman now and must make the best of it."

"You are a very impertinent old businessman," said the earl. "So what are you offering in return for my distinguished presence? Free meals? Half price?"

"I am not offering cut rates of any kind, my lord. Our hotel speaks for itself. Either you choose to suffer here or you come where the atmosphere is elegant, and the food a veritable poem."

The earl opened his mouth to refuse but at that moment one of the Corinthians, the one with his muddy boots on the chair, spat noisily on the floor.

"Perhaps I will accept your offer after all," said the earl faintly. "But I will inspect the accommodation first."

"Gladly," said Sir Philip, creaking to his feet, creaking because he was laced into a new Apollo corset, a vanity which had brought down the scorn of Lady Fortescue on his head. She had pointed out that the fatter his love became, paradoxically the thinner Sir Philip seemed to wish to appear.

***

Sir Philip found it pleasant to be in favour again as he handed over his trophy in the form of one elegant earl to Lady Fortescue and the colonel.

The earl declared himself satisfied with the apartment and said he would send his man for his luggage. This proved to be quite a considerable amount even for such a notable as a handsome earl, a fact which puzzled the poor relations, for they had been asking about and no one could remember the earl's having favoured London much in the past, preferring his estates in the country, which hardly made him a Fashionable. Just before dinner, Sir Philip returned with the intelligence that the earl, although in his early thirties, was a widower. His wife had died four years ago and it was romantically assumed that he had gone into deep mourning for her, although a great deal of luggage in a London hotel suggested the dandy. Certainly the earl was exquisitely dressed, and yet there was little of the fop about him. He did not wear paint and his hair was all his own. At first Sir Philip had said waspishly that such glorious hair must be a wig, and only when the earl was seated at the best table in the dining-room—the Poor Relation boasted separate tables instead of communal long ones—that Sir Philip, by dint of staring very hard at the back of the earl's head through his quizzing-glass, admitted finally that the hair was real.

The earl looked up as two guests entered the room. The lady, he noticed, was hardly anywhere near the bloom of youth and yet was dressed like a débutante in a white muslin gown with puffed sleeves. The young miss with her looked familiar, and he was sure he had seen her before and recently. This was borne out by the fact that she gave him a slight and surprised smile of recognition before following her mother, who was in turn being led by Colonel Sandhurst to a table in the corner.

The waiting at table by these aristocratic owners of the hotel, which was much vaunted, consisted, the earl noticed, of Sir Philip, Lady Fortescue and the colonel courteously serving a few plates of soup and then they contented themselves with supervising the work of the waiters.

The food was excellent. The earl made a good meal but could not help noticing that the schoolgirl miss with the wide hazel eyes only picked at hers. He would have been amazed had he known that he was the reason for her loss of appetite.

"Do try to eat your food," Lady Carruthers was saying. "It is not like you to be so nice."

"How would you know, Mama?" asked Arabella. "I cannot remember the last time we dined together."

Even in London, before the roof fell in, Arabella had been expected to eat her meals in the schoolroom there, just as she ate her meals alone in the schoolroom at home.

"I wonder who that extraordinarily handsome man is,"

mused Lady Carruthers. She raised an imperious hand and summoned Lady Fortescue, who looked at her thoughtfully and who in turn summoned Sir Philip, who advanced on Lady Carruthers.

"Yes, my lady?" demanded Sir Philip testily. He wanted to be with his beloved next door, not creaking around the dining-room being summoned by an under-dressed doxy, which was how he privately damned Lady Carruthers.

"Tell me, who is that handsome gentleman over there?"

"That is the Earl of Denby."

"Thank you, you may go."

This high-handed dismissal was enough to put Sir Philip's back up. He turned to Arabella. "You have made a poor meal of it," he said. "Can I perhaps get you something else?"

"No, thank you, Sir Philip," said Arabella, whose innate courtesy had prompted her to find out the names of the owners of the hotel. "This food is indeed excellent. I am a trifle out of sorts."

"Then after dinner I shall send our Miss Tonks to you. She is excellent at brewing possets, having learned the recipes from our Mrs. Budley."

"That will not be necessary," said Lady Carruthers, but Sir Philip had turned on his heel and walked away.

Denby, thought Lady Carruthers. Estates in Denby-shire, prosperous; wait a bit, married. No, wife dead; I remember taking note of that. Early thirties, yes, but I look like a young miss.

She smiled at her daughter. "I saw the earl look this way. He probably thinks we are sisters."

Her eyes were glowing. Arabella realized with a sinking heart that her mother was about to pursue the man of her, Arabella's, dreams.

CHAPTER TWO

It's a very odd thing—
As odd as can be—
That whatever Miss T. eats
Turns into Miss T.
Porridge and apples,
Mince, muffins and mutton,
Jam, junket, jumbles—
Not a rap, not a button
It matters; the moment
They're out of her plate,
Though shared by Miss Butcher
And sour Mr. Bate,
Tiny and cheerful,
And neat as can be,
Whatever Miss T. eats
Turns into Miss T.
         —WALTER DE LA MARE

*L*ady Carruthers had retired to bed, but Arabella was sitting reading in the small sitting-room allotted to them when Miss Tonks was admitted and asked if there was anything she could do to help Miss Carruthers.

Miss Tonks was fashionably dressed in rustling brown silk shot with gold. Her sheeplike face was earnest and non-threatening, so Arabella smiled and said that Miss

Tonks was most kind but there was nothing she required.

At that moment Lady Carruthers opened her bedroom door and demanded waspishly if Arabella meant to keep her awake all night chattering with the servants, and then slammed the door with force.

"I do apologize," said Arabella, flushing slightly, "Mama is a trifle fatigued."

"I find," said Miss Tonks hesitatingly, "that an impairment of the appetite is often caused by worry or love. I myself have been eating badly lately. But I must not keep you talking, although"—she looked shyly at the floor—"we have a charming sitting-room upstairs and there is no one there at the moment, if you would like a comfortable coze."

If Arabella had said no at that point, her life might have turned out differently, but intrigued and amused, she stood up and said, "Lead the way, Miss Tonks."

When they reached the "staff" sitting-room, Miss Tonks ordered tea and cakes, for she wondered if Miss Carruthers's dreadful mama might have something to do with the girl's loss of appetite.

"Is anything worrying you at the moment?" asked Miss Tonks when they were seated in front of a bright but tiny fire.

"I do not think I am exactly worried about anything," said Arabella cautiously. "But you did say that your own appetite was bad because of worry. I am not in the way of talking to anyone, but that makes me a good confidante."

Miss Tonks looked doubtfully at the young face, the girlish dress and the long hair.

"I am nineteen," said Arabella with a quaint dignity.

Miss Tonks hesitated, but only for a moment. She missed her friend, Mrs. Budley. The desire to unburden herself was great.

"Did you mark Sir Philip Sommerville?" she began.

"The elderly gentleman, yes."

Miss Tonks gave a faint sigh. "Yes, he *is* elderly, I suppose. When my friend Eliza Budley married recently–she was part-owner here–Sir Philip and I went to the wedding in Warwickshire. We had a great adventure on the road there. A highwayman stopped our coach and our coachman and groom ran away. I shot him, and Sir Philip was so proud of me instead of being waspish and unkind as he usually is. On the road home, we were very friendly, very close, and like a fool, I began to dream of marriage."

"But is there not a great distance between your ages?" asked Arabella, who correctly judged Miss Tonks to be in her forties.

"Oh, yes, a *vast* difference, my dear. But you see, I am become so weary of being a spinster. At your age, one dreams of handsome young men, and then, later on, perhaps of someone of the same age, then of a widower, and then, I suppose when all hope has fled, anyone will do. It was then that Sir Philip, while we were companionable together at an inn in Chipping Norton, yes, Sir Philip, he read in the newspapers that the Prince Regent had been a guest in the dining-room. He became incensed. He thought Colonel Sandhurst and Lady Fortescue should somehow have got news to us, although, as they did not know where we could be found, I do not know how he could have expected them to manage. But he was in a foul temper all the way to London and he threw a scene when we got here and stormed off. He came back with Mrs. Mary Budge, a coarse and common widow-woman with a huge appetite. He said she would help us but she does nothing but sit and eat and yet he can find no fault with her. He looks at me with all the old scorn. I ... I cannot bear it."

Miss Tonks began to cry quietly. Arabella perched on the arm of the spinster's chair and gave her a hug. "You surely deserve better than the attentions of an old rake. Come, Miss Tonks, I have *seen* Sir Philip. He looks like a tortoise."

Miss Tonks gave a faint giggle and dried her eyes just as Jack, the footman, entered with a tea-tray. When he had left, Miss Tonks composed herself and poured tea, noticing with satisfaction that Arabella had started to eat the cakes with every evidence of a healthy appetite. "I have made such a fool of myself," said Miss Tonks shyly.

"Not at all," said Arabella. "I am not versed in the ways of the world, but you are obviously too much of a lady to be pining away over such as Sir Philip. Still, if you need help, help is what you will have. Perhaps a plan of action would help. Have any of you seriously tried to dislodge this Mrs. Budge?"

"No, not really. Lady Fortescue has insisted that he pay all Mrs. Budge's bills, but even that does not seem to move him to get rid of her."

"I read a lot," said Arabella simply. "I shall think of something."

"And what of you, my dear Miss Carruthers? What has happened to affect *your* appetite?"

"The Earl of Denby."

"The handsome earl? You have met him before?"

"Not before today, Miss Tonks. I have not been in the way of meeting people and Mama is looking for a new husband—Papa died a year ago—and so she thinks if she keeps me looking like a school miss, then she will appear younger. I did not mind before today. I am used to a solitary life. But when I was standing at the window of our town house, I saw the earl arrive to pay a call on the neighbours. He ... he looked like all the heroes in the books I read. I regret to say I read a great number of romances. I asked Mama when I could make my come-out, for then, you see, I would have a chance to talk to him, perhaps to dance with him." Her large eyes grew wistful. "But Mama is coming out herself, so to speak, and I fear she will fail to find a husband, and so the years will pass until I look like a freak in these clothes."

"But he is *here* in this hotel, Miss Carruthers. You will have many opportunities to get to know him."

"He will not notice me. Or, if he does, he might pat me on the head and give me a toy. What hope do I have, looking like this?"

"You are no longer alone," said Miss Tonks, her kind heart touched. "May I please tell my partners about your hopes? Sir Philip is so resourceful." She blushed. "Well, he is. He may be horrible most of the time and a genuine antique, but he is amazing at plotting."

"You are most kind." Arabella looked worried. "But I think such as Lady Fortescue would find the romantic thoughts of a young woman a trifle ridiculous."

"I do not think so. Besides, they would not tell anyone else and they would not make you feel silly."

"In other words, I must have as many recruits to my cause as possible?"

"Oh, exactly. Believe me, this hotel was started because of a group of us who no longer wanted to be alone and poor. That is why it has such an odd name. We did expect at the beginning, you know, that our angry relatives would buy us out, but that did not happen and now Lady Fortescue enjoys the business so much that she will not really consider selling it and I ... I have nowhere else to go."

Arabella looked at her sympathetically and said, "My mother cannot really interfere with any plans, for she leaves me alone for most of the day, and the evening too. Last night was about the only time she has ever dined with me. And with the possibility of the earl being in the dining-room, she will make me eat my meals in my room."

"She cannot do that," said Miss Tonks. "We do not serve meals in the rooms."

"Then no doubt she will send the footman out to a chophouse. When should I consult the others?"

"Three o'clock tomorrow would be a good time," said Miss Tonks.

Arabella sat and quietly ate another cake before standing up to take her leave. "Until tomorrow. One last favour."

"Anything in my power."

"Would you please call me Arabella? No one does except Mama, and that does not count. I would like a friend."

"Then you may call me Letitia."

Arabella left and Miss Tonks sat down again, a little glow of warmth beginning to spread through her thin body. She had a friend, and such a young friend, too.

In the office in the morning, a surprised Lady Fortescue listened to Miss Tonks's tale of the ambitions of Miss Arabella Carruthers.

"I sympathize with your desire to help the child," she said. "But although you say she is nineteen, there is still the age difference. Besides, the earl is a widower. He has been married. I do not yet know if there are any children by that marriage, and yet ..."

"But," interrupted Miss Tonks eagerly, "even if it is impossible to make a match for Arabella with the earl, and in the clear light of day, I think it is, we could at least perhaps think of some plan to encourage Lady Carruthers to bring her out. To that end, I have invited Arabella to join us at three this afternoon. She has volunteered to try to think of a way of dislodging Mrs. Budge."

"You seem to have become remarkably *cosy* with her. And on such a brief acquaintanceship, too."

"Despite her years, she seems kind and wise, and she has asked me to call her Arabella."

"How touching." But Lady Fortescue's thin lips curled in a smile. She had been worried of late about the lowness of Miss Tonks's spirits and was glad to see her with a new interest.

Sir Philip walked in. He saw from the chill in Lady Fortescue's eyes that the warmth towards him engendered by his securing the Earl of Denby had quite gone. Miss Tonks looked at him sadly and that aggravated Sir Philip's temper. "What's up with you, moo-face?" he demanded.

"My many failings in appearance are as nothing when compared to the shabby vulgarity of your inamorata," countered Miss Tonks.

"Enough," said Lady Fortescue. "Sir Philip, you brought Mrs. Budge into our establishment on the clear understanding that she would help with the chores. It is time she started."

"I shall ask her to wait table in the dining-room tonight," said Sir Philip.

Lady Fortescue repressed a shudder. "That woman is as common as a bum-bailey. She would no doubt eat what any of the guests left on their plates. She can attend to the guests in their rooms. Miss Tonks will show her what to do."

Miss Tonks let out a bleat of dismay. "But we do not need her, Lady Fortescue. She would only become over-familiar with the guests."

"If she fails in these simple duties," said Lady Fortescue, ignoring the spinster, "then she will be put to the kitchens to help Despard and Rossignole." Despard and Rossignole were the two French chefs whose creations had made the Poor Relations the talk of the town.

"That precious pair do not brook interference in their kitchen," pointed out Sir Philip.

"I grow tired of this." Lady Fortescue's black eyes bored into Sir Philip. "Tell your lady to report for duty."

Sir Philip exited with as near a flounce as his bent figure and crablike walk could achieve. He stood in the hall under the constantly burning candles in the great chandelier which he had tricked his nephew into giving him. The chandelier swung slightly in the draught and prisms of light from the crystals floated across Sir Philip's tense face. He was dreading telling Mrs. Budge that she had to work. And yet, why should he worry? he wondered. She had never been other than placid and warm-hearted. He was sorely in need of money. Now that Mrs. Budge's bills could no longer be lost in the general hotel bills, it meant he would need to find extra money. He considered briefly thieving from the guests, but shrank from it. Since they had all turned honest, even he could not bring himself to return to crime.

He made his way to the apartment next door. His love was sleeping in a bed in the corner of the sitting-room, the sitting-room having been commandeered for her use. She was lying on her back, snoring. For one brief moment, he saw her as the others saw her. But then she turned in her sleep and her huge breasts spilled over the top of her night-gown. He untied his cravat and prepared to join her, all thoughts of money or getting her to work forgotten for the time being.

* * *

Miss Arabella Carruthers waited anxiously for her mother to wake up and go out so that she could join the hotel owners in their sitting-room. Her mother did not rise until one or two. Would she be gone by three? Arabella fretted. The day had started badly. She had been amusing herself by walking up and down the stairs and along the hotel corridors, wondering what it had looked like when it had been a private house. A child had run out of one of the rooms, chasing a bright ball. Arabella had tried to stop it, but the ball had run past her and down the stairs. "I'll get it for you," she called gaily. She ran down the stairs and then stopped short. The earl was standing there, holding the ball in his hand.

Miserably conscious of her girlish appearance, Arabella tried to be as stately as possible. She curtsied low. He smiled and held the ball out to her. She took it and thanked him. She was about to try to start up a conversation when he said, "The pleasure is mine," and ruffled her hair. She turned and scrambled back up the stairs like the child he obviously thought her to be, her face flaming with mortification. She gave the ball to the child and returned to the apartment to brood.

To her infinite relief, at precisely a quarter to three her mother sallied forth to make calls after many agonizing complaints that this fan would not do and these gloves were the wrong colour.

When she entered the "staff" sitting-room at precisely three o'clock, Lady Fortescue was saying, "That woman never put in an appearance. Really, it is too bad." She looked up and saw Arabella. "Welcome," she said. "We have not introduced ourselves formally. I am Lady Fortescue, to your left is Colonel Sandhurst, and Miss Tonks you already know. Tea will be served shortly."

Arabella curtsied and sat down. "You must excuse us, Miss Carruthers," said Lady Fortescue, "but we have a certain domestic problem we are anxious to discuss, particularly as Sir Philip Sommerville is absent."

"The problem of Mrs. Budge? I have been considering that," said Arabella.

The colonel looked at her indulgently, his eyes twinkling.

"My dear, I do not think you have met such as Mrs. Budge in all your life."

"But I have a *plan*," said Arabella eagerly. "I was awake quite a bit of the night thinking it out."

"Very well," said Lady Fortescue, although she cast a fulminating look at Miss Tonks. What had that lady been about, enlisting the help of a young miss?

"It's this," said Arabella. "Sir Philip is very old." Three pairs of eyes glared at her. "I m-mean," she faltered, "I do not think Mrs. Budge can be in love with him."

"Granted," said Lady Fortescue. "The woman is a leech. Go on. Ah, tea."

Arabella waited impatiently until Jack, the footman, had deposited the tea-things on the table, and retired.

"It is like this," she said eagerly. "You must offer this Mrs. Budge a richer victim."

"Who?" Lady Fortescue was obviously becoming increasingly impatient.

"You could pay some actor to masquerade as a rich merchant and to court her. That would dislodge her from Sir Philip."

There was a long, considering silence, broken at last by Miss Tonks. "My dear Arabella," she said, "I do believe it might work."

Arabella turned bright eyes on Lady Fortescue.

"It just *might* work," said that lady consideringly. "What do you think, Colonel?"

"The trouble is that we usually leave that sort of organization to Sir Philip. He would find a suitable actor."

"I have been thinking," said Miss Tonks, "that it is time I developed bottom. Perhaps if there were some way I could go to the theatre with Miss Carruthers, then we could survey the cast and pick out someone suitable and approach that gentleman in the Green Room after the performance."

"Perhaps," ventured Arabella, "it might be better to find some actor who is not in employ and would do anything for some money. I read an article in the newspapers last year about the coffee-houses of London and it said that the players met in John's Coffee-House in Drury Lane."

"I shall go there directly," said the colonel and then they all looked at each other in surprise, surprise that Arabella had hit on a solution to their problem, surprise that the retiring colonel of all people had accepted the idea so readily.

"Two ladies visiting an actor in the Green Room would occasion comment," added the colonel.

Lady Fortescue dispensed tea and then turned to Arabella. "Now to your problem, Miss Carruthers. Perhaps we must find a way to alter your appearance. I think, were you allowed to look your age, then perhaps Denby would favour you. First things first. Ah, I have it. Miss Tonks, you were saying the other day that you wished to have your hair arranged by Monsieur André."

Miss Tonks nodded.

"Perhaps if you could wait a little longer. We could summon Monsieur André, making the appointment for mid-afternoon, when Lady Carruthers is out on calls or in the Park. We get him to give Miss Carruthers a fashionable crop—"

"All that beautiful hair!" exclaimed the colonel. "Why not just get it put up?"

"Because put-up hair can be taken down again. We explain that Monsieur André made a terrible mistake and should have done Miss Tonks's hair instead. Lady Carruthers will be furious, but we will ask why she is so angry that her daughter's hair has received such an expensive crop and at the hotel's expense. The lady can hardly say it is because she wishes to appear young herself that she keeps her daughter looking as if she had just come out of the schoolroom."

"I saw the earl this morning," said Arabella miserably. "I was chasing a ball which a child had thrown. I ran down the stairs to get it. He picked it up and he ... he ruffled my hair."

"Oh, dear," said Lady Fortescue. "I think we will send Jack with an order to Monsieur André, but first, Miss Carruthers, you must make sure he calls—or rather, that we arrange for him to call—when Lady Carruthers is guaranteed to be out of the hotel."

"I will look at her cards," said Arabella eagerly. "I think she is to attend the Pattersons's ball tomorrow night."

"I doubt if such a famous personage as Monsieur André can come at such short notice," remarked Lady Fortescue, "but we can try."

The colonel got to his feet. "I will go to John's Coffee-House. If I find a suitable actor, I will bring him back here directly."

"No, Sir Philip might see him. Arrange for him to call after dinner, when Sir Philip will have retired with his slut."

***

The colonel walked to Covent Garden, to Drury Lane. Although not a vain man, he could not help stopping to admire his appearance in a looking-glass in a shop window. He looked so different from the shabby individual who had collapsed from hunger at Lady Fortescue's feet in Hyde Park. His morning dress of corbeau-coloured coat, striped waistcoat, buff breeches and glistening top-boots had restored his outward appearance to that of a gentleman of fashion. But he could not help wishing he were actually a gentleman again instead of a man in trade.

He gave a little sigh and went on his way, his cane tucked under his arm at just the right angle, his new beaver hat tipped rakishly over his pomaded white hair.

When he reached the coffee-house, he hesitated in the doorway, suddenly made timid by the company. Some had come from rehearsals and were highly painted. All appeared to be gesticulating and talking at the tops of their voices. Some brandished tattered scripts.

His blue eyes ranged from one face to another and at last came to rest on the disconsolate figure of a slight middle-aged man who was sitting alone in a corner. He had a thin, sad face and liquid brown eyes and thick brown hair dusted with grey. His clothes were shabby and his shirt-points were frayed.

The colonel made his way over to this individual's table. "May I sit here, sir?" he asked.

"By all means." His voice reassured the colonel, who felt it was an actor's voice, the vowels well-rounded, the tone mellifluous.

The colonel ordered a bottle of wine and two glasses. "Forgive the liberty, sir," he said, addressing the actor. "I do not care to drink alone. Will you join me?"

"Gladly. I am Jason Davy."

"Player?"

"Yes, indeed."

"I am Colonel Sandhurst, at your service."

"And what is Colonel Sandhurst doing in a players' coffee-house?"

"Mr. Davy, I am looking for an out-of-work and hungry actor."

Mr. Davy looked at him ruefully. "I am out of work and very hungry."

The colonel signalled to the waiter and ordered a meat

pie and vegetables. "You will feel better when you have eaten something, Mr. Davy. Nothing clouds the judgement more than hunger."

The actor looked at him consideringly. "You must have been in some hard campaigns in your life, Colonel, to know what hunger is like."

"It was not in the army that I came to know hunger," said the colonel quietly. While they drank and waited for Mr. Davy's food, the actor pointed out various personages and talked about the plays they were appearing in.

The colonel explained he was part-owner of the Poor Relation Hotel in Bond Street and told various harmless but amusing stories about hotel life while the actor ate, cleaning every bit of food from his plate.

"Now, sir," said Colonel Sandhurst, "I will explain our problem. One of our partners, Sir Philip Sommerville, has fallen in love with a widow, a Mrs. Mary Budge, who is greedy and grasping and brings discredit to our establishment. We do not believe she has one genuine spark of affection for Sir Philip. Accordingly, we hit on this plan. If we could engage the services of an actor to appear in the guise of a wealthy merchant, someone who could court Mrs. Budge and dislodge her from the hotel, we would be free of her."

The actor's hands swept down his shabby clothes in an eloquent gesture. "I am hardly in a position to look like a rich merchant."

"Suitable clothes can be bought for you and you will be given expenses above your fee to woo this creature."

Mr. Davy leaned back in his chair. "Colonel Sandhurst, if you can see your way to finding me a cheroot, I am your man."

The colonel took out a squat leather case and laid it on the table. "Take what you want, sir."

Mr. Davy snapped open the case. He took out six

cheroots, five of which he stowed about his person. How wonderful, thought the colonel, to be so unselfconsciously poor. He himself in the days of his poverty had often longed for a cheroot but would never have dared ask for one, let alone help himself to six of them.

The actor lit a cheroot from the candle on the table, puffed out a cloud of smoke and leaned back in his chair.

The colonel smiled at him, his blue eyes twinkling. "Now we will discuss terms, Mr. Davy."

* * *

They stayed the rest of the afternoon, drinking coffee, the colonel pointing out that they would need clear heads and that Lady Fortescue did not appreciate the company of bosky men. By early evening, the colonel ordered a substantial dinner for both, and by the time he and Mr. Davy sauntered out into the streets of London, the colonel had the odd feeling that he had known Mr. Davy for quite a long time. Mr. Davy was grateful for the food, the wine, the cheroots and the work and emanated an aura of simple and grateful affection which was most endearing. He appeared to have accepted the new role he was about to play with equanimity.

"I have been thinking," said the colonel, idly watching a child driving a dogcart down Drury Lane with all the expertise of a member of the Four-in-Hand Club, "that it would be better if you were resident in the hotel. As we only cater for aristocrats, and you in the guise of an aristocrat would be far above Mrs. Budge's touch, I will describe you as the son of a friend of mine from my regimental days who has made a fortune in the City. Can you talk business matters enough to convince Sir Philip?"

"Oh, I think so."

"Remember, Sir Philip is a downy one."

"And the other partners, they know about this masquerade?"

"Yes. Both Lady Fortescue and Miss Tonks have agreed to it."

"And was it your idea, sir?"

The colonel idly speared a cabbage leaf with his stick as they walked through Covent Garden and then flipped it away. "No, the plan was the idea of a Miss Carruthers, daughter of Lady Carruthers, who is staying at the hotel. Lady Carruthers is a widow. I believe her husband, Sir James, died a year ago on the hunting field. This daughter was befriended by Miss Tonks. Miss Carruthers is forced to dress as a school miss although she is nineteen because her mother is on the hunt for husband number two and wishes to look younger than her years."

"Like a play," mused the actor as they strolled amiably together in the failing light under the flickering parish lamps. King Street, New Street, across St. Martin's Lane, Cecil Court, Bear Street and so to Leicester Square and on to Piccadilly. London was at its best at this time of night, with the still-open shops glittering with treasures from all over the world and with the air full of the smells of fruit and spices. Traffic was quieter in the West End, as the various nobles who owned parts of this quarter of the Town had put posts and barriers at strategic parts so that they would not be disturbed too much by the rumble of any carriages other than their own.

"Bond Street at last," said the colonel.

"I often come here," said Mr. Davy. "It is a street of dreams. Here one can imagine one is rich, an adventurer, part of the fashionable throng."

The colonel led the way into the hotel, handed his hat, gloves and cane to Jack and led the way up the stairs.

The three ladies had been waiting impatiently for his return, that is, Miss Tonks, Lady Fortescue and Arabella, with Lady Fortescue beginning to have serious doubts whether the colonel would succeed in his mission.

They looked up in relief as the colonel entered the sitting-room and then curiously at the shabby actor who followed him.

With an air of triumph, the colonel introduced Mr. Davy, who swept them all a magnificent bow.

"Mr. Davy is prepared to play his part," said the colonel, explaining that the actor was to masquerade as a rich Cit.

"He will need to stay in his lodgings until suitable clothes are ready for him," said Lady Fortescue.

"I could rent some suitable clothes," said the actor.

Lady Fortescue shook her head. "No, Mr. Davy, stage clothes will not fit the part. Sir Philip is very sharp, and there must be no smell of grease-paint about you. Miss Tonks, give this dish of tea to Mr. Davy. A cake, Mr. Davy? They are our chef's best. His choux pastry is a miracle. You seem a kind and amiable man, Mr. Davy. But have you got it in you to woo a gross and vulgar woman such as Mrs. Budge?"

"If Mrs. Budge is as Colonel Sandhurst describes her," said the actor, "then she is greedy and after money, so my charms will not be much needed."

Miss Tonks leaned forward, her eyes shining. "The theatre fascinates me. I would love one day to go backstage and to see how all the scenery works."

Mr. Davy smiled. "I could easily take you any time you want. I may be out of work, but I am still one of *them* and can come and go in the playhouse during rehearsals as I please. Perhaps tomorrow afternoon, if you are not otherwise engaged ...?"

"I would love to go as well," said Arabella.

"Wait a bit," said the colonel, alarmed. "Mr. Davy is going to have to keep clear of this hotel until his clothes are ready and then he is going to have to pay attention to Mrs. Budge and to no one else."

"But we could meet him at the theatre," begged Miss Tonks.

"There is the matter of Miss Carruthers's hair," put in Lady Fortescue. "Monsieur André will be here tomorrow evening."

"That's tomorrow afternoon then," said Mr. Davy. "I will meet both of you at the stage door in the Haymarket at two o'clock."

Arabella's face fell. "Mama does not rise until two. She does not go out on her calls until three at the earliest."

"Then we will make it three o'clock," said Mr. Davy easily, and helped himself to another cake.

"I know who you are," shrieked Miss Tonks suddenly, making them all jump. "You were Rosencrantz when Kean was playing Hamlet; let me see, that would be in 1802. I was in the gallery, but I marked you particularly. Jason Davy. Yes, and you played Mirabell a year later, in *The Way of the World.*"

Mr. Davy dusted icing sugar from his fingers and grinned. "My greatest moment." He stood up and took up a position by the fireplace and declaimed, "Her follies are so natural, or so artful, that they become her; and those affectations which in another woman wou'd be odious, serve but to make her more agreeable. I'll tell thee, Fainall, she once us'd me with that insolence, that in revenge I took her to pieces; sifted her, and separated her failings; I study'd 'em, and got 'em by rote. The catalogue was so large, that I was not without hopes, one day or other to hate her heartily. To which end I so us'd my self to think of 'em, that at length, contrary to my design and expectation, they gave me every hour less and less disturbance; 'till in a few days it became habitual to me, to remember 'em without being displeas'd. They are now grown as familiar to me as my own frailties; and in all probability in a little time longer I shall like 'em as well."

He finished and sat down to a spattering of applause. Lady Fortescue reflected that it was some time since she had seen Miss Tonks look so happy and animated. Her thin rouged lips curved in a sudden smile. "Well acted, Mr. Davy. Pray do have another cake."

***

While the late tea-party was taking place in the Poor Relation, the Earl of Denby was sitting in his club, talking to his friend, Mr. Peter Sinclair, who had just arrived in Town. "So how do you plan to amuse yourself?" asked Mr. Sinclair.

The earl smiled lazily. "Oh, this and that. Nothing very strenuous. A few out-of-Season balls and parties, perhaps a visit to the playhouse."

"As to that," said Mr. Sinclair, blushing slightly, "there is to be a performance of *The Way of the World* in the Haymarket. Very fine. Mrs. Tarry plays the part of Mrs. Millamant. Have you ... have you seen Mrs. Tarry?"

"No, I have been a country bumpkin for a number of years now."

"Ah, she is such a delicate creature. Such wit! Such charm! I go to rehearsals and sometimes she ... she smiles on me. I am going tomorrow afternoon." He fished in his pocket. "I bought her this," he said, bringing out a flat red morocco case. "Tell me what you think."

The earl took it and flicked open the case. A thin string of sapphires set in gold sparkled up at him.

"I am not surprised Mrs. Tarry smiles at you if you give

her geegaws like this. Is there a Mr. Tarry, or is the "Mrs." a courtesy title?"

"Oh, some bad-tempered lout of an actor. I do not mark him."

"May I be vulgar enough to suggest that your wife, Joan, might be a trifle distressed were she to know of your infatuation?"

"Pah, the country has made you old-fashioned and staid. Mrs. Sinclair has her friends and interests—"

"Not to mention seven children," murmured the earl, thinking, not for the first time, that somehow Peter Sinclair had never grown up. He still looked like an overgrown school-boy with his unruly mop of black curls and ingenuous face.

"If you had ever been in love," began Mr. Sinclair hotly and then broke off, looking ashamed of himself. "Forgive me, I had forgotten the sad death of your wife."

The earl nodded, his face a well-bred blank. "Go on. Tell me how you met Mrs. Tarry."

"I saw her in *Macbeth*. Her performance as Lady Macbeth was better than that of Mrs. Siddons, I assure you. A friend took me backstage. We looked at each other. She said nothing but I felt, in that moment, our souls were joined."

Practised flirt, thought the earl cynically, and one used to getting jewels from naïve men like Peter. "Perhaps you would care to introduce me to this paragon?" he said.

Mr. Sinclair brightened. "I will take you tomorrow to the rehearsal. You are a cold fish and you think yourself immune to the softer passions."

"Now did I ever say such a thing?" asked the earl, amused.

"No, but I am a good judge of character. But mark my words. Love may be waiting for *you* in the theatre tomorrow!"

***

Arabella went to bed that night but was unable to sleep. She thanked God for bringing her to this hotel which had changed her lonely life. She wondered what she would look like with her hair cropped. She got out of bed and lit a branch of candles with a taper and carried it over to the mirror at the toilet-table. She put down the candles and then sat down and twisted her hair on top of her head, turning this way and that. And would the earl notice her after Monsieur André had finished with her?

She blew out the candles and sighed and returned to bed and began to make up a scenario where the earl would see her coming down the stairs with her new hair-style and he would clutch his heart and his eyes would shine. She fell asleep, and in her dream, the earl ruffled her hair and said, "Well, Arabella, and what do you think of your new papa?" And her mother said, "Congratulate us, my love, Denby and I were married by special licence this morning, and we have already picked out someone for *you*, Denby's little brother." They stood aside and revealed a low-browed, pocked-face man who leered at her and his hairy hands reached out for her.

Arabella screamed and sat up in bed, her heart thumping. She must ask the hotel owners to find out whether the earl had a brother.

CHAPTER THREE

Anger helps complexion,
saves paint.
—WILLIAM CONGREVE

Sir Philip felt uneasy next day. Something was going on, something that excluded him. Miss Tonks had told him of the plan to crop Arabella's hair and Lady Fortescue informed him that the Dessops had been about to leave without settling their bill but that Colonel Sandhurst had handled the matter beautifully.

Although he had often complained in the past that he was the one who had to sort out all their problems, he had enjoyed the attention and now he felt old and useless. Also there was an *atmosphere*, an air of suppressed excitement. They were up to something, he thought, and that something did not include him.

In order to try to win his way back into Lady Fortescue's good graces, he returned to the flat next door and roused his beloved and told her she was expected to help as chambermaid in the hotel.

"But o' course, sweetheart," she said, shifting her bulk against the pillows. "But my back is somewhat sore. I've always had trouble with my back. Perhaps if you could get Despard to send over some of his jellied chicken, it would help me to recover."

For once Sir Philip showed no interest in her health. "I did bring you here, Mary," he said, "on the understanding that you would be one of us and help to run the hotel."

"I know you did, light o' my life. But what's to do? They all hate me." And she began to cry.

Alarmed, he went to soothe her. He could not very well tell her that all loved her when he knew the dearest wish of the others was that she would leave. The others might see her as a gross and grasping woman, but to Sir Philip she was generosity and warmth itself. And so, while he dried her tears, he missed seeing Miss Tonks and Miss Carruthers leaving in a hired carriage to go to the theatre.

Arabella was as excited as the child her mother fondly hoped she looked like. She did, however, wish she had a new gown, a new grown-up gown. Miss Tonks had found a very smart straw bonnet embellished with flowers which Mrs. Budley had left behind and had presented it to Arabella, and that was a comfort. Arabella had established that her mother would definitely be absent when Monsieur André called, and as her mother always took her maid and footman with her, Arabella was comfortably confident that there would be no one around to stop Monsieur André's cutting her hair. She had not seen the earl, but she wanted him to see her next with her fashionable new crop. It was wonderful to dream, she thought cynically, because in dreams one could write the play and set the scene and make one's heart's desire say all the lovely things one wanted to hear him say.

Not being accustomed to any friends at all, she was humbly grateful for Miss Tonks's warmth and interest. Having led a loveless life herself, Miss Tonks was only too happy to become involved in Arabella's hopes and dreams.

Miss Tonks did experience a little pang of dread. This visit
to the rehearsal meant so much to her that she feared that Mr.
Davy might not be there. Besides, it had begun to rain, dreary
English, soaking rain. The carriage slowed and jolted forward in
fits and starts. It was amazing that on a dry, sunny day, carriages
sped over the London streets like so many gilded dragonflies,
but when it rained, everything ground to a surly halt and
coachmen swore at each other, horses steamed and stamped,
and the air was redolent of garbage and horse manure. But as
they finally arrived at the theatre, it was to see Mr. Davy shel-
tering in the doorway and looking anxiously for them.

"You are a trifle late," he cried, "but no matter. What a
smart bonnet, Miss Carruthers! Please follow me, ladies. We
can watch a little of the rehearsal from the wings."

How proud they were of this shabby actor who had the
power to lead them into the enchanted world of backstage.
How grandly did Mr. Davy nod to the surly doorkeeper as he
led them in at the stage door. With what ease and familiarity did he conduct them through the labyrinthine passages
towards where they could hear the sound of the actors'
voices. And then they were there, among the towering flats;
and there, in front of the footlights, stood the actors.

In the rehearsal, the character of Lady Wishfort was
at her toilet, berating her maid, Peg. She was played by a
Mrs. Leigh, Mr. Davy whispered to them. Mrs. Leigh's voice
reached them clearly.

"'I have no more patience—If I have not fretted myself 'till
I am pale again, there's no veracity in me. Fetch me the red—
the red, do you hear, sweetheart? An errant ash colour, as I'm
a person. Look you how this wench stirs! Why dost thou not
fetch me a little red? Didst thou not hear me, mopus?'"

The maid came into their line of vision, saying, "'The

red ratifia does your ladyship mean, or the cherry brandy?'"

Lady Wishfort again. "'Ratifia, fool? No fool. Not the ratifia, fool. Grant me patience! I mean the Spanish paper, idiot, complexion darling. Paint, paint, paint, dost thou understand that, changeling, dangling thy hands like bobbins before thee. Why dost not thou stir, puppet? Thou wooden thing upon wires.'"

Arabella shifted uneasily. Lady Wishfort reminded her forcibly of her own mother preparing to go out for an evening and tormenting her maid.

It was a very "warm" play, thought Miss Tonks, and perhaps not one that she should have taken Arabella to see. And yet it was so funny, and none of the characters came out with anything coarser than Sir Philip did when he was in a rage.

The rehearsal was finally over. Mr. Davy led the way to the Green Room. Mrs. Tarry, the leading actress, took her place on a sofa in the centre of the room. Several very grand gentlemen were paying court to her. She was still in greasepaint and costume, a costume cut so low it exposed the tops of her nipples.

Perhaps the finest thing about her were her eyes, which were very large and dark brown and which she used to great advantage. And then those eyes widened and filled with warmth. The actress held out a hand and cried, "My dear Mr. Sinclair."

Arabella caught hold of Miss Tonks's hand and held it tight. For following this Mr. Sinclair into the pool of light around the sofa cast by a tall candelabrum strode the Earl of Denby, hat held in one hand. "Mrs. Tarry, allow me to present my good friend, the Earl of Denby, who expresses himself as smitten by your charms."

The earl raised Mrs. Tarry's hand to his lips and Arabella felt all her dreams shatter. But the earl, having paid his respects, obviously felt he had done his part. He turned round and saw a slim girl with long hair down her back under a fetching straw bonnet standing beside a thin, spinsterish lady. He frowned a little and then his face cleared. The child from the hotel, looking vastly pretty in a grown-up bonnet.

Miss Tonks whispered to Mr. Davy, who was on the other side of her, "Is there any way you can engineer an introduction for Miss Carruthers to Lord Denby?"

"Obliquely," he said. "Come forward."

He led them into the circle of light and bowed low. Mrs. Tarry leaped to her feet with genuine enthusiasm. "Jason Davy," she cried. "Where have you been?" Arabella reflected that despite his boast, Mr. Davy did not go backstage these days as much as he had led them to believe.

"Oh, here and there, my heart," said Mr. Davy. "May I present my two friends, who are vastly enamoured of your performance? Miss Tonks and Miss Carruthers."

Miss Tonks forgot she was there to further her friend's marital ambitions. She looked at the actress with glowing eyes and said, "You are wonderful! Such grace, such elegance!"

And Mrs. Tarry, who did not normally have much time for women, glowed before this praise and smiled at Miss Tonks and introduced the circle of men. The earl nodded to them and then said to Arabella, "You are staying at the same hotel as I, are you not?"

"Yes, my lord," said Arabella.

"And are you enjoying the play, child? Does your mama know you are frequenting the Green Room of a theatre?"

"I am nineteen years old, my lord, and no, my mama does not know I am here. But I am not in the way of having friends or of going anywhere, so I beg you will not tell her."

"That is hardly likely to happen as I do not have the pleasure of being acquainted with your mother."

"Oh, but you will," said Arabella and bit her lip in confusion.

"And why so confident, miss?"

Arabella felt she had gone far enough. She could hardly say that as her mother was looking for a husband and because the earl was an eligible man, her mother would soon effect an introduction. Where were all the light and clever things she had rehearsed in her mind? She hung her head and blushed.

Miss Tonks moved to the rescue. "I am a part-owner of the Poor Relation, my lord," she said. "I trust you are comfortable."

"Extremely, ma'am." He looked at Arabella. "And is Mrs. Carruthers one of the owners as well?"

"*Lady* Carruthers is a guest."

The earl's interest was aroused. This pretty girl with her large eyes and long, long hair was Lady Carruthers's daughter. Lady Carruthers could not know her ingénue was consorting with a shabby actor and a spinster who helped to run the hotel. Out of the corner of his eye, he could see his friend, Mr. Sinclair, down on one knee, presenting that necklace to Mrs. Tarry. He said quickly, "Perhaps I could take you all for some ices or a dish of tea, Miss Tonks?"

"Thank you," said Miss Tonks, much gratified. "We should like that above all things."

"Do you have your carriage?"

"Yes, my lord."

"Then shall we meet in Berkeley Square at Gunter's in, say, half an hour?"

"Delighted," said Miss Tonks. "Your lordship is *too* kind, so *very* kind."

The shrewd Mr. Davy saw the earl was already regretting his invitation and quickly drew Miss Tonks away. "Leave it be," he muttered, "or he'll change his mind."

He took Arabella and Miss Tonks on a brief tour of the backstage, showing them the scenery and the dressing-rooms, before hustling them out to the carriage.

"I wish I had waited," mourned Arabella as the carriage lurched forward in the rain. "How can I engage his interest when I look so unfashionable?"

"You must seize the opportunity when it arises," said Miss Tonks firmly. "Is that not so, Mr. Davy?"

"Oh, yes."

"What were these men doing in the Green Room?" asked Arabella.

"Most of 'em were paying court on Mrs. Tarry," said Mr. Davy. "And I think that Mr. Sinclair, the earl's friend, hopes to make her his mistress. Just before we left, did you notice that necklace he gave her?"

"And were they all looking for mistresses?" asked Arabella in a small voice.

"No, they usually go to the opera for that," remarked Mr. Davy, staring out at the rain. "The dancers at the opera are much in demand."

"Do you think Lord Denby has an opera dancer?"

Mr. Davy sat up straight, alarmed. "Hey, it don't do for any female to be talking about a man's opera dancers, and don't you forget it."

Arabella relapsed into gloomy silence. Opera dancers had not featured in any of the wonderful plays she had written in her head about herself and the earl. Although, from over-hearing her mother's gossip to her friends, she was well aware that many men had mistresses, it was very lowering to think that the man of her dreams might have one as well.

This idea began to plague her so much that when they arrived at Gunter's to be welcomed by the earl and ushered to a table, she could think of nothing else. Mr. Davy and Miss

Tonks had agreed to converse with each other just before the carriage arrived at Gunter's so as to leave Arabella free to talk to the earl. So as soon as they were comfortably seated, Miss Tonks turned immediately to Mr. Davy and began to question him about the theatre.

The earl looked at Arabella's expressive face and said gently, "Something is troubling you, Miss Carruthers?"

Those large eyes of hers fringed with long lashes studied his face and then she said quietly, "I was wondering if *you* had an opera dancer?"

For one moment his face froze. He was about to resort to the aristocratic tactic of appearing to become immediately deaf, but again his curiosity stabbed him.

"I have not been long resident in London, Miss Carruthers," he said. "I have not had time. But when I get around to it, would you like me to let you know?"

"I do not know what came over me," said Arabella miserably. "I am terribly indiscreet. You see, my lord, as you will observe from my childish dress, I am kept mostly in the schoolroom and do not get about much and ... and ... perhaps if I had a little Town bronze, I would not make such disgraceful remarks."

"You are forgiven, Miss Carruthers. But why are you kept in the schoolroom? There is no schoolroom at the hotel, so I assume you were speaking figuratively."

"Yes, I was. Papa died last year and we are in London for Mama wishes to find a husband. Having a grown-up daughter is a disadvantage and so ... Oh, I have done it again. I should not have said that. Oh, dear, there is something else!" She looked at Mr. Davy.

"What now?" asked the earl indulgently, thinking that to feel interested and amused was an unusual state of affairs for him these days.

"Miss Tonks," cried Arabella. "Lord Denby should not have met Mr. Davy!"

Miss Tonks and Mr. Davy looked at Arabella in dawning consternation.

"Now why should I have not met Mr. Davy?" asked the earl. He added maliciously, "Can it be that Mr. Davy and Miss Tonks are having a secret liaison?"

"My lord!" Miss Tonks' sheeplike face was crimson.

"I am sorry," he said, not looking sorry at all. "But Miss Carruthers has infected me with bluntness. Perhaps you had better explain what you mean."

Miss Tonks struck her bosom. If the earl had been infected by Arabella's bluntness, then Miss Tonks had been infected by the theatre. "We must throw ourselves on your mercy, my lord."

"I shall tell him," said Arabella firmly. "I have already broken the rules of polite conduct. My lord, Sir Philip Sommerville is part-owner of the hotel."

"I have met the gentleman."

"He has become enamoured of a vulgar woman, a Mrs. Budge, who does nothing but eat. Miss Tonks, Colonel Sandhurst and Lady Fortescue—that is, the other partners in the hotel—want rid of her for she is a leech, but Sir Philip is besotted."

"Are you sure?" The earl's blue eyes sparkled. "Sir Philip is as old as Methuselah."

"One is never too old to be a fool," said Miss Tonks bitterly.

"So," pursued the earl, "what has Mr. Davy here to do with this?"

"Well, you see, it was Arabella who hit upon a plan," said Miss Tonks.

"Arabella?"

"Miss Carruthers. She suggested that we should hire an out-of-work actor to masquerade as a rich merchant. In the guise of a merchant, the actor, Mr. Davy here, would then court Mrs. Budge. We are convinced that Mrs. Budge's interest in Sir Philip is purely mercenary. If she saw better game, then she would detach herself from Sir Philip *and* the hotel. But the trouble is, having met Mr. Davy you would recognize him in his guise of rich merchant and perhaps say something."

"What an enterprising young lady Miss Carruthers is," laughed the earl. "If you are not out in the world, Miss Carruthers, where do you get your ideas from?"

"Books, and my own imagination," said Arabella. "But you will not betray us, my lord, for we amuse you ... for the moment."

"No, you have the right of it. And what of yourself, Miss Carruthers? Surely with such a fertile brain you can hit on a plan to get your mother to bring you out?"

"Oh, Lady Fortescue has already thought of something," said Arabella. "It was to be a surprise ..." She bit her full bottom lip. She had been about to say, "It was to be a surprise for you."

"Anyway," she went on, "Miss Tonks here had expressed a wish to have her hair done by Monsieur André, the famous hairdresser. Lady Fortescue has invited him to the hotel tonight while Mama is at the Pattersons's ball. He will give me a fashionable crop and Lady Fortescue will tell Mama that the hairdresser made a mistake."

"Yes, it would be a mistake," said the earl slowly. He looked at the glory of Arabella's shining brown hair. Because the day was dark, the candles on the tables had been lit and Arabella's hair gleamed with faint auburn lights. "Cannot you just get it put up?"

"Put-up hair can be brushed down again," pointed out Arabella.

"Perhaps I can think of something." They all watched the earl anxiously. Lady Carruthers, reflected the earl, was obviously a heartless and tiresome woman on the hunt for a husband. It was a wonder she had not dressed up this beautiful girl to look her best so as to attract men. That is what a lot of the old harridans did. He brightened. Perhaps if Lady Carruthers could be persuaded that her daughter was useful bait, then she might come about.

But although Miss Carruthers was cynical about her mother, she might not appreciate such plain-speaking.

"Your mother has not had an opportunity to appreciate your worth, Miss Carruthers," he said. "I am at loose ends at the moment. In fact, Town wearies me and I wish I had not come. But your schemes delight me. What if I were to pretend to court you, Miss Carruthers? Surely that would open Lady Carruthers's eyes."

Miss Tonks could see the flash of pain in Arabella's eyes, could see that she was about to refuse, but a pretend courtship could lead to a real one. "What a good idea," said Miss Tonks loudly. "You may feel a trifle embarrassed at the moment, Arabella, but *think on it.*"

Arabella studied the spinster in silence and grasped what it was Miss Tonks was silently trying to communicate. If she allowed the earl to court her, then she would see him. If she refused, he might amuse himself by going off to find an opera dancer. "Oh, very well," she said, a trifle ungraciously.

"And in return," said the earl, "do not have your beautiful hair cut."

Although it was dark and rainy outside, Arabella suddenly felt as if the room were filled with sunlight. No one had ever complimented her before. "I would suggest then," she said to Miss Tonks, "that you cancel the hairdresser because Lord Denby cannot start to court me right away, and if Mama sees my hair up, she will immediately get her maid to brush it down, and all that money will have been spent for nothing."

"I am going to the Pattersons's ball tonight," said the earl. "I will dance with Lady Carruthers, which will give me an opportunity to call on her tomorrow and meet you."

"If Mama knows you are to call, then she will send me out with the maid," said Arabella.

"Ah, then I shall appear suitably disenchanted and so she will expect me to send my servant instead." It was the custom for gentlemen to call the next day on ladies they had danced with the night before, but many sent their servants if they were not particularly interested in their dancing partners.

Mr. Davy looked at the clock on the wall and gave an exclamation of surprise. "I am to meet the colonel and go to his tailor."

They all rose, Arabella with a feeling of regret. The earl looked down at her curiously, wondering what she would look like with a modish hair-style and fashionable clothes. He saw her turn slightly pink under his steady gaze and gathered his wits. He had come to London, complete with new clothes, to find a wife, a wife who would bear him sons and enliven the solitude of his life in the country. Playing games with a young miss was not the way to go about it, and yet there was something endearing about Arabella Carruthers and the odd company she kept.

At his club later, before he returned home to change for the ball, he was accosted by Mr. Sinclair. "Well, what did you think?" asked Mr. Sinclair. "Is she not ravishing, divine?"

"A pretty-enough actress, I'll grant you that, but I fear Mrs. Tarry may prove expensive."

"She has a mind above material things," exclaimed Mr. Sinclair. "And what of you? Who were those odd people you left with? That shabby actor, the drab middle-aged creature and the baby."

"The baby is Miss Arabella Carruthers, daughter of Lady Carruthers. She is, in fact, all of nineteen years."

"How odd! What an odd way to dress! Does she make her come out at this unfashionable time of the year?"

"I do not know," said the earl, affecting boredom. "Talk of something else."

And Mr. Sinclair was only too happy to return to rhapsodizing about the beauties of Mrs. Tarry while the earl followed his own thoughts. His marriage had not been a success. It had been an arranged marriage, arranged for him by his father before the old earl died. His wife, Henrietta Babbington, had seemed well enough, and arranged marriages were very common. He had not thought much about love, but often, when the prattle of his wife's conversation irritated him, and when she lay at night as passive in his embrace as a dead body, he had often regretted following his family's wishes. For most of the marriage she had been ill. He had suspected her of manufacturing illness. She lay, day in and day out, in a darkened room, surrounded by patent medicines. She was addicted to dosing herself with mercury, a medicine which was just beginning to go out of favour. Whether it had been the mercury or whether she had, after all, been really ill, he did not know, but when she died, he suffered from extreme guilt, feeling that he could perhaps have done something to get her out into the fresh air, to rally her spirits. He had then worked hard on his estates, believing in a way that he had no right to enjoy himself.

Recently he had begun to find himself free of guilt and determined to get back into the world and enjoy himself. His clothes had become sadly old-fashioned even in an age when fashion moved slowly, and so he had ordered a great many new ones from the best tailor. But London appeared such a boring, affected sort of place, or at least it had seemed like that until that afternoon.

When he left Mr. Sinclair and returned to the hotel to change, he looked at it with new eyes. It was well-appointed and well-run. He was suddenly curious to know more about the owners and how they had started out.

***

Lady Fortescue, when told about the afternoon and the earl's plan, said that they must be careful that his intentions towards Arabella were honourable, and Miss Tonks pointed out that with the girl's mother in residence, they could hardly be anything else, although, at the moment, she added, the earl did not look on Arabella in a romantic light, merely seeing her as an amusement, a diversion.

Colonel Sandhurst was beginning to report on his visit to the tailor with Mr. Davy when Sir Philip came in with Mrs. Budge. Sir Philip's pale eyes darted this way and that. He had heard the sound of the colonel's voice as he had approached the door of the sitting-room, a voice that had broken off and fallen silent the minute he entered. Secrets, he thought. They have secrets which don't include me.

He realized Lady Fortescue was speaking. "Sir Philip," she said, "we are as usual delighted to see you, but unless your companion is here to offer her services in some capacity, I must ask you to take her away."

"Mary's going to start work tomorrow," said Sir Philip, "and I'll thank you to treat her with respect."

"Why?" demanded Lady Fortescue. "Her very presence is an insult to us."

The door of the sitting-room opened and Arabella slipped quietly in.

"See here," said Mrs. Budge truculently, "you've got no right to be so high and mighty wi' me. You ain't nothing but a load o' tradespeople."

"Sir Philip," said the colonel quietly, "this sitting-room is our refuge, and we would be obliged if you would escort your lady out."

"Oh, you would, would you?" demanded Sir Philip wrathfully. "Well, so I shall, and I shall be back in a trice to tell you lot something that'll make your eyes start out o' your stupid heads."

"Now what?" demanded Lady Fortescue after Sir Philip had propelled the bulk of his lady from the room. "There is no insulting that creature. By which I mean she is determined to stay and batten on us."

"Perhaps it might be better to tolerate the woman," said Arabella, "until our plan goes into action. You might goad Sir Philip into doing something silly."

"Like what?" asked the colonel.

"Like demanding all his share of the hotel and going off and marrying Mrs. Budge."

"I do not think he would do that," said Lady Fortescue. "He has extravagant tastes and any money he got from his share would soon be dissipated. Now, Miss Tonks, I forgot to cancel Monsieur André's visit and he will be here presently, and as you expressed a wish to have your own hair done, perhaps you should make use of his services."

"So soon?" Miss Tonks's thin hands fluttered up to her brown hair, which she wore under a cap.

"Why not?" said the colonel heartily. "You deserve a treat."

"When is he due here?"

"In half an hour," said Lady Fortescue.

"But he is such a great man and my bedchamber is so small."

"You can use Mama's room," said Arabella. "She will not be home until dawn, and by that time I shall have certainly removed all traces of the hairdresser's visit."

Miss Tonks made up her mind. "Then I shall do it. Will you come and sit with me, Arabella?"

"Gladly."

Lady Fortescue experienced a pang of sympathy for Miss Tonks. The spinster was so obviously delighted to have a friend, and yet, a pretty girl like Arabella would soon marry and Miss Tonks would be left alone again. Strange that Sir Philip's romance should have affected her so badly.

They talked then about general things and menus, none of them anxious to return to the subject of Mr. Davy when Sir Philip was expected to return.

At last he came in and stood looking contemptuously around the room, jingling coins in his pockets. He then noticed Arabella and raised his eyebrows in surprise, but then his gaze returned to Lady Fortescue and the colonel. "You've all gone too far," he said. "So hear this. I am going to marry Mary Budge."

"No!" screamed Miss Tonks.

"Fiddle," said Lady Fortescue.

"You can't," said the colonel bluntly.

"I can and I will," declared Sir Philip.

"Has she accepted you?" asked Lady Fortescue.

"No, ain't asked her yet. But she will. She knows which side her bread is buttered on."

"That one likes her bread buttered on both sides, and loaves and loaves of it, too," said Miss Tonks with a break in her voice.

"And what's more," went on Sir Philip who, Arabella

noticed shrewdly, seemed to be enjoying himself immensely, "I think I'll get you to give me my share in this hotel. Fed up working. Want to be a gentleman."

Miss Tonks rose to her feet. "Nothing," she said passionately, "could *ever* make you a gentleman!" She marched from the room, her head high, two spots of colour burning on her cheeks. Arabella followed her.

"Come down to Mama's apartment," said Arabella.

Miss Tonks shook her head blindly. "Why ornament an old fool like me?"

"Because it will make you feel better," said Arabella quietly. "You are already a distinguished-looking lady, Letitia. I would like to see what Monsieur André does with your hair. And I'll tell you something else. I do not think Sir Philip is going to propose to Mrs. Budge."

"But he said ..."

"He said it to get revenge on all of you, firstly because he really does care for that awful woman, but secondly because he smells secrets from which he is excluded. He is like a bad child, I think. Come along."

* * *

The earl was dancing with Lady Carruthers. He was glad it was a country dance, for the few times the figure of the dance brought them together caused her to ogle him in quite a dreadful way and so it was easy for him to show coldness to her. And hard as she worked at flirting, Lady Carruthers' spirits were plunging by the minute. The earl was the first gentleman who had asked her to dance and she feared he would be the last that evening. She could not see what she really looked like when she surveyed herself in the glass. She still saw herself as young as her clothes. And yet there was no denying that her dreams of being surrounded by eligible men were falling about her ears. Instead of sitting with the chaperons and dowagers, she had taken a place with the young débutantes. That had been a mistake, for as each was taken up to dance, she was left alone on her rout-chair, feeling exposed. She could have crossed the room and joined friends of her own age, but she felt that by so doing she would draw attention to her age. Of course London was thin of company, but it was mortifying after all these years to find herself a wallflower. When her dance with the earl was over and they were promenading around the room, she said with an arch look, "I look forward to your call tomorrow, my lord. As we are both resident in the same hotel, I feel confident that you will call in person."

"I doubt if that will be possible," he said loftily. "I have many engagements." And with the next dance being announced, he led her back to that lonely seat.

***

The fashionable crop that was to have been Arabella's was now adorning Miss Tonks's head. "What do you think?" she asked nervously after the hairdresser had left.

Arabella put her head on one side. "You know," she said consideringly, "it makes you look *years* younger, and I wonder what he used to get that shine. I asked him but he said it was a secret recipe."

Miss Tonks's hair was now a cap of shining curls. "And you should not wear these starched caps," went on Arabella. "Some pretty lace ones, I think, to show those curls to advantage. Come upstairs with me and let us see if the others are still there."

The others were still there, going through the books, Sir Philip's face looking sour. "So you say," Lady Fortescue was declaiming in a measured voice, "as we have no intention of selling up, you will be only entitled to your cut of the profits, profits from which your lady's food and clothes and rent have been deducted. You are an extravagant man, Sir Philip, and so I do not think you would be able to exist very comfortably in a separate establishment."

"A pox on't," muttered Sir Philip. "What's this girl doing here again? Is she to be party to all our discussions?"

"Miss Carruthers is a friend," snapped the colonel. "Mind your manners, sir!"

Sir Philip's gaze focused on Miss Tonks's capless, shining head. "What have you been doing to yourself?" he growled.

The colonel took Miss Tonks's hand and bent and kissed it. "You look most charmingly."

"I must say," remarked Lady Fortescue, "that André has done wonders. How very young you look, Miss Tonks!"

"Pah!" said Sir Philip Sommerville, and went out and crashed the door behind him.

"He does not like you looking pretty," Arabella whispered to Miss Tonks. "I wonder why?"

And Miss Tonks, who had been on the point of crying, suddenly felt very happy indeed. No one in her whole miserable life had called her pretty before.

Lady Fortescue, who had overheard the aside, reflected that no one could ever call Miss Tonks pretty, and yet the new hair-style made her look undoubtedly interesting and mundane.

***

"Did many gentlemen dance with you last night, Mama?" asked Arabella. For to her dismay, early the next afternoon, her mother showed every sign of preparing to go out on calls.

"Oh, so many I have lost count," said Lady Carruthers.

"In that case, would it not be better to await calls rather than going out?"

"Oh, there was no one of interest, no one worth waiting for."

"Was Lord Denby there?"

"Denby? Denby?" Lady Carruthers affected a yawn and tried to look as if she were hard put to remember the name of the only man who had danced with her. "Oh, yes, the fellow who is staying here. Yes, he danced with me. Terrible flirt."

The footman came into the sitting-room. "The Earl of Denby is called, my lady," he announced.

"Show him in," said Arabella quickly before her mother could order her from the room.

The earl, reflected Arabella, although her heart gave a painful lurch, was surely as good an actor as Mr. Davy. He came in and bowed low to Lady Carruthers. Then he turned and affected to see Arabella for the first time and gave a little start.

"I pray you," he said to Lady Carruthers, "please introduce me to this beauty."

Lady Carruthers looked wildly about the room as if expecting to see someone else there. "Arabella?" she asked faintly. She rallied with an obvious effort. "My daughter, my lord. Arabella, make your curtsy to his lordship and then I am sure you will be glad to get back to your books."

But the earl had taken Arabella's hand and was smiling down into her eyes. "You must not waste your beautiful eyes over books, Miss Carruthers." He turned back to Lady Carruthers. "May I persuade both of you to come for a drive with me?"

"I shall be glad to go," said Lady Carruthers. "But my child is ..."

She saw the slight stiffening of Lord Denby's face and

realized with a shock that he might, just might, change his mind if Arabella were not to be of the party.

"Arabella, change into your carriage dress, my chuck, while I entertain Lord Denby."

When Arabella had gone into her bedroom, Lady Carruthers said, "Such a dear child."

"Not a child, my lady, despite her juvenile gowns. I would have estimated her to be about nineteen years."

Lady Carruthers coloured under her paint but said nothing.

"Have you brought her out yet?"

"No, my lord, this is not the Season."

"And yet, with such beauty, you would have the men flocking around her—were she suitably gowned, of course. And she is trifle old to be still wearing her hair down."

"Oh, let us not discuss my tiresome child," said Lady Carruthers gaily. "I confess I am fatigued. So many dances!"

Lord Denby restrained himself from pointing out that apart from one dance with him, she had not danced at all. He talked about various people they both knew, for most of society at least knew one another by sight and by gossip, while Lady Carruthers fretted as the minutes dragged by, wondering what on earth her daughter was about, to take so long to put on her carriage gown.

The door from Arabella's bedroom opened and she entered followed by Lady Carruthers's worried-looking maid. Lady Carruthers's eyes looked daggers.

Arabella was wearing one of her own, that is, Lady Carruthers's, own carriage gowns, and one of her mother's best hats. And worse! For under that dashing little hat her hair was piled up on her small head in shining curls and waves. The earl smiled his appreciation. Arabella was transformed into a beautiful and modish young lady.

They made their way down the stairs to the hall. Miss Tonks was standing there, talking to one of the guests. She saw the party approaching and cried, "Arabella! How very fine you look."

Lady Carruthers gave Miss Tonks a contemptuous look. "You will kindly be less familiar with my daughter. I do not like familiarity from hotel servants."

"Good day, Miss Tonks," said the earl easily. "Your hair looks splendid, very fetching."

"Is Letitia not grand," cried Arabella. "But then, Monsieur André is the very best."

Nonplussed and feeling that life was treating her very unfairly, Lady Carruthers made her way to the door but found to her mortification that she had to wait there alone while the earl and her wretched daughter finished talking to that wretched hotel woman. She was bewildered. Arabella, she kept thinking. Is Arabella then so very beautiful? I never noticed.

When they were seated in the earl's carriage, she kept darting little looks at her daughter from under the shadow of her bonnet. For the first time Lady Carruthers was bitterly jealous of her daughter. Her own face was a mask of paint; her daughter's, free of paint, glowed with good health. Not one line marred that beautiful face opposite, and the hazel eyes were wide and clear. On the other hand, the earl had called to pay his addresses. Lady Carruthers preened. All her vanity, which had taken a sad blow at the ball, came flooding back. Once more she saw herself as irresistible and began to flirt with the earl so that he had little opportunity to speak to Arabella. Had Lady Carruthers allowed him plenty of time to get to know Arabella better, then the earl might have tired of the game. But the fact that his every move to engage Arabella in conversation was thwarted by her mother made him more intrigued by the girl.

"Your daughter is attracting all eyes," said the earl as they drove in the Ring in Hyde Park.

But Lady Carruthers's vanity was fully restored and she thought it was charming and kind of the earl to flatter her little daughter so as to please *her*. After all, Lady Carruthers knew that it was obviously herself that all the men in the Park were admiring.

CHAPTER FOUR

*What woman, however old,
has not the bridal favours and raiment
stowed away, and packed in lavender,
in the inmost cupboards of her heart?*
—WILLIAM THACKERAY

The earl found himself feeling increasingly frustrated. He had initially made up his mind that when Lady Carruthers started to take her daughter out and about, he would favour the girl with a few dances and then forget about her. But during the following two weeks, only Lady Carruthers herself was present at various social functions. At last, after flicking through his cards, he noticed there was to be a musicale on the following night, hosted by a Mrs. Sinclair. He approached that lady and said that he had learned Lady Carruthers had a very pretty daughter also staying at the Poor Relation and perhaps Mrs. Sinclair might oblige him by sending a note to Lady Carruthers saying that her daughter would be welcome also.

Mrs. Sinclair smiled indulgently, assuming the earl to be smitten with Miss Carruthers, and said she would send a note right away.

Lady Carruthers scowled down at that note. She felt she

was making progress with the earl. Into every indifferent remark he had made to her she read growing passion. Then he always asked her to dance and the fact that he always asked about Arabella she considered a very hopeful sign. The earl obviously had a fatherly interest in the girl. And so she shrugged and crumpled up the note and threw it into the empty fireplace.

Arabella found it later that day, smoothed it out and read it. She was feeling increasingly angry because her mother showed no signs of wanting to take her anywhere and doubted very much whether she would take her to this musicale. Also Arabella was weary of wandering the corridors of the hotel hoping to bump into the earl. Her mother did not even take her to the dining-room but had her meals sent in from a chop-house.

The only thing that brightened her days was the fact that Mr. Davy's clothes had been made at great speed and he was to arrive in his new guise the next day. Lady Fortescue had decided it would get him closer to Mrs. Budge if, instead of staying in the hotel, he stayed at the apartment next door, which would also underline the fact that he was the son of a friend of the colonel's.

The following evening, Arabella wistfully watched her mother getting ready to go out. Arabella was going to go up to the "staff" sitting-room the moment her mother disappeared to judge how well Mr. Davy was playing his part. It had been decided to let him keep his own name, as Sir Philip never went to the theatre and Mr. Davy had not trodden the boards for some time. Sir Philip, she knew, had gone off with Mrs. Budge to her flat which she had rented out because the tenant was behind with his payments, but Lady Fortescue had left a note for him telling him to be in the sitting-room at ten o'clock.

As soon as her mother had left, Arabella put her hair up

and took a fashionable gown out of her mother's wardrobe and put it on. She would look like a young woman for this one evening, although the only people to appreciate the result would be the poor relations.

The gown she had chosen was of thin white muslin ornamented with sprigs of forget-me-nots. It showed off her excellent figure to advantage, although it was slightly tight across the bosom. She had a Norfolk shawl draped around her shoulders and some of her mother's perfume behind her ears. She had been modestly pleased with her reflection in the glass, and as she left the room she wistfully thought that it would be wonderful if the earl could meet her and see her in all her grown-up glory.

She walked to the main staircase and met the earl, who was dressed to go out in black evening dress, sculptured cravat and hair pomaded so that it shone like gold.

He automatically bowed and then his eyes widened. "Miss Carruthers! You look so very charming. You will break all hearts tonight."

Arabella laughed. "You mean Sir Philip might transfer his attentions to me?"

He frowned. "But I understood that you were to attend Mrs. Sinclair's musicale. In fact, Mrs. Sinclair told me that she would send a note to Lady Carruthers suggesting you attend."

Arabella gave a rueful little shrug. "I found that note crumpled in the fireplace and Mama said nothing of it to me, so here I am, but looking forward to the first meeting of Mr. Davy and Sir Philip."

He felt a sudden spasm of anger against the absent Lady Carruthers and then found he was not looking forward to the evening at all. On impulse, he said, "I would like to attend the first act of this play. Do you think Lady Fortescue would mind?"

Her eyes lit up. "No, for Miss Tonks has already told her that you know of the plan. But Mama will be expecting to see you."

His blue eyes danced and he held out his arm. "I think you deserve to enjoy yourself thinking about her disappointment. Shall we go?"

She put her hand on his arm and he led her up the stairs.

When they entered the sitting-room, Arabella's eyes immediately searched the room for Mr. Davy. "He is not here yet," said Lady Fortescue. "Why, my lord, to what do we owe the pleasure of your visit?"

"I was anxious to see Mr. Davy's performance and Miss Carruthers was sure you would not mind."

"Delighted to have your company, my lord," said Lady Fortescue smoothly, although her shrewd black eyes fastened on the transformed Arabella. The girl was a trifle young for Denby, she reflected, but Miss Tonks was looking as happy as if she had created this new Arabella herself and Lady Fortescue reflected that anything that made Miss Tonks happy these days was worth her indulgence. Not that she wanted to see anything of a romance between Miss Tonks and Sir Philip should the dreadful Budge creature disappear. Sir Philip had certain ... em ... appetites, thought Lady Fortescue, which might shock a genteel virgin.

The door opened and Mr. Davy came in. "Splendid! Oh, how splendid!" said Miss Tonks, clapping her hands.

Clothes had transformed the actor from a shabby player into a smooth and elegant gentleman. From his well-tailored evening coat to his silk breeches and clocked stockings to his new and fashionable Brutus crop, he looked like a wealthy man without a care in the world.

"Your servant," he said, bowing low before the colonel.

"Jewels," said the earl. "You must have jewels, Mr. Davy.

That will attract Mrs. Budge's greedy eyes. I will fetch something."

He left the room and returned some minutes later with a diamond stickpin, a large ruby ring and diamond studs. "The studs in your shirt," ordered the earl. "Quickly now. Perhaps you would be so good as to help him, Miss Tonks; your assistance would be welcome."

Mr. Davy was bedecked just in time. Sir Philip entered with Mrs. Budge, holding her hand high above his head, as if the pair were about to perform a minuet.

Sir Philip stared in surprise at the earl and said rudely, "What's he doing here?"

"Lord Denby," declared Lady Fortescue repressively, "is escorting Miss Carruthers. My lord, may I present Mrs. Budge."

"So charmed," fluted Mrs. Budge in a crimped-up sort of voice.

"And Mr. Davy here is the son of an old friend of Colonel Sandhurst who will be residing with us. Mrs. Budge, Mr. Davy. Sir Philip, Mr. Davy. Mr. Davy, Mrs. Budge and Sir Philip Sommerville."

To Arabella's surprise, Mr. Davy gave Mrs. Budge a low bow but did not show any signs of being interested in her at all.

"Where are you from, Mr. Davy?" asked Sir Philip.

"I now live in Buckingham," said Mr. Davy, "but I like to visit the City from time to time to see my man of business."

"Business doing well?" asked Sir Philip.

"Very well. I wish Colonel Sandhurst had told me of your venture at the beginning. I would have been glad to help."

"And why didn't he?" demanded Sir Philip crossly, thinking the colonel had kept this rich friend well hidden.

"Colonel Sandhurst and I had become disaffected owing to my behaviour," said Mr. Davy. "I fear I was a very wild young man. But now I have made my fortune, I had an impulse to come to beg his forgiveness."

"Hey, sit by me," said Sir Philip expansively, his eyes fixed on that diamond stickpin. "Any friend of Colonel Sandhurst is a friend of mine."

"I had heard of Lady Fortescue, Miss Tonks and Sir Philip from Colonel Sandhurst," said Mr. Davy. "Are you a partner, too, Mrs. Budge?"

Mrs. Budge had taken a place on his other side. She was reaching out one plump hand for a cake. "I am by way of being a friend of Sir Philip," she said.

Arabella saw Mr. Davy's lips move in a whisper and then the actor said aloud, "Allow me to hand you the plate of cakes, Mrs. Budge." She saw how Mrs. Budge after that whisper had given Mr. Davy a gratified look and then how her piggy eyes fell from the actor's face to the diamond nestling among the snowy folds of his cravat.

"I don't think I will have a cake, sir," simpered Mrs. Budge. What Mr. Davy had whispered to her when she had said she was a friend of Sir Philip had been, "Oh, my heart. What a pity. What a waste." The import of these words had sunk into her ample bosom. Mrs. Budge was suddenly aware of her own great girth set against the elegant slimness of Mr. Davy and resolved to eat less, just a little less.

"Sir Philip!" commanded Lady Fortescue. "Join us for a moment. There appears to be a discrepancy in the accounts."

"As Miss Tonks has been doing the accounts lately, I am not at all surprised," said Sir Philip. "That widgeon cannot even add two plus two."

Arabella saw anger flash in Mr. Davy's eyes, but Miss Tonks said, "Don't be such an old fool, Sir Philip. If there is any discrepancy in the accounts it is no doubt you, sir, trying to hide your extravagance."

Sir Philip sat down beside Lady Fortescue, took out his quizzing-glass and examined the accounts.

"It is a while since I have been in Town," said Mr. Davy quietly to Mrs. Budge. "I miss female company. My poor wife died some years ago. She never lived to see me make my fortune."

Mrs. Budge looked thoughtfully at the cake plate so temptingly near and restrained herself with an effort. "Well, sir," she said archly, "I am sure when Sir Philip is busy about his duties I could find time to accompany you, although perhaps, on second thoughts, he might not like it."

Mr. Davy's eyes danced wickedly and he murmured, "Then we shall not tell him, madam. Now I have rented a handsome carriage and thought to take the air at two o'clock tomorrow."

Mrs. Budge felt like Cleopatra. Her breath began to come and go quickly. "If you was to take me up just outside Lord Nelson's old house down the street, then that would not be offending a certain gentleman."

"And what do you think that was all about?" whispered Arabella to the earl. She leaned close to him and he could smell her perfume.

"I think everything is going splendidly," he whispered back.

But Miss Tonks noticed that Sir Philip, closing the accounts book with a snap, had his pale eyes fastened on the couple in a speculative way. The old man's brain was obviously working at a great rate.

"Sir Philip," said Miss Tonks, "have you found any error?"

"No, I haven't, mophead."

"Don't be rude," said Miss Tonks with a new confidence given by the smart crop covered with a dainty lace cap. "You must admit I do the figures very neatly. And why are you so nasty about my hair?"

He crossed over to her and put his head on one side. "You look very well," he said gruffly. "I'm old and I don't like change of any kind."

"No more do I," said Miss Tonks, looking sadly at Mrs. Budge.

Sir Philip experienced a rare pang of conscience. He had no right to be so nasty to Miss Tonks when she had saved his life by shooting that highwayman on the Fosse in Warwickshire. And she *had* changed. No one could ever call her pretty, but Miss Tonks had a certain air of breeding and elegance which... He looked at Mrs. Budge and his brain snapped down on the thought. He was old and was entitled to a few pleasures. And who was this Mr. Davy who had sprung from nowhere?

"Oh, you have a pianoforte," exclaimed Arabella. "Is that a new purchase?"

"Yes," said Lady Fortescue. "Colonel Sandhurst bought it second-hand the other day in the fond hope that I would play to him; but it is years since I have played anything. Miss Tonks confesses to being a poor performer, and so it remains silent, which is probably just as well. It has obviously not been tuned this age and is sadly tinny."

"What about you, Miss Carruthers?" asked the earl.

"I play very well," said Arabella and then blushed. "I do not mean to brag, but it is the *only* thing I do well."

"There are sheets of music on top of the piano, which came with it," said the colonel eagerly.

Arabella crossed to the piano followed by the earl, who lit the candles in their brackets with a taper. "I will turn the music for you," he said.

Suddenly nervous, for she was not used to an audience, Arabella chose a ballad and began to play. "I know that one," said Sir Philip and began to sing in a surprisingly strong baritone. Miss Tonks joined in with a reedy soprano, and after an amused look back at them, the earl began to sing as well.

When that ballad was over, Mrs. Budge heaved herself to her feet. "My turn," she said. "Do you know 'Lizzie of the Strand'?"

"I am afraid not," said Arabella, "but I can follow a tune very easily."

So Mrs. Budge began to sing in a distinctly ginny voice.

> *"Sweet Lizzie walked along the Strand,*
> *Tol rol, diddle dol,*
> *Her garters in her hand,*
> *For Captain James had had his way,*
> *And—"*

"And that's enough of that!" Lady Fortescue's voice cut across Mrs. Budge's singing. "If you are going to sing like that, then I suggest you get to Billingsgate, where you belong."

"Enough of your insults," raged Sir Philip. "Apologize."

"My turn," said Mr. Davy, crossing to the piano. He riffled through the sheets of music. "Ah, this one."

He began to sing "Sweet Maiden With Your Eyes Divine" in a clear tenor. Sir Philip slowly resumed his seat. The man was a brilliant performer. The angry emotions ebbed out of the room. Miss Tonks sat with her hands clasped and her eyes shining. The earl suddenly noticed how white and fine Arabella's hands were and how long her eyelashes. He became more determined than ever to find some means of forcing Lady Carruthers to bring her out.

Mr. Davy finished his song by sinking down on one knee in front of Mrs. Budge to loud applause.

"You are wasted in the business world, sir," commented Sir Philip. "You should have trodden the boards."

"How silly you are," said Miss Tonks quickly. "A gentleman like Mr. Davy a common actor! Fie for shame!"

Sir Philip shrugged dismissively and then turned to Mrs. Budge. "I suggest we retire."

She hesitated a moment and then decided it would be best to humour Sir Philip by removing herself from Mr. Davy or she might not be able to escape to meet him on the morrow.

When they had gone, Mr. Davy looked ruefully around the company. "I apologize for my performance. I overdid it. It will not happen again. But Mrs. Budge is to come driving with me tomorrow afternoon, so I fear you will have the expense of renting a carriage."

"Oh, excellent," said Lady Fortescue. "How did you manage it? I heard nothing."

"I saw you whispering in her ear," said Arabella, amused. "And now to my problems. Lord Denby here persuaded a Mrs. Sinclair who was giving a musicale this evening to write to Mama and ask her to bring me, but she did not, as you can see. Nor does Mama know that I am wearing one of her gowns."

"Does not the pretend courtship of Lord Denby persuade her to take you about?" asked Lady Fortescue.

"On the contrary," said Arabella. "Mama is now convinced that Lord Denby is courting *her*."

The door opened and Sir Philip walked back in again. "Mrs. Budge has a headache," he said sourly and sat down. Mrs. Budge had decided that leaving with Sir Philip was enough but letting him in her bed that night was too much. She wanted to be alone and dream about Mr. Davy, or rather, Mr. Davy's money. "What are you lot plotting?" asked Sir Philip suspiciously.

"We are wondering how to persuade Lady Carruthers to bring Arabella out," said Miss Tonks.

Sir Philip looked at them thoughtfully and then said, "We'll bring her out ourselves."

"My dear sir!" Lady Fortescue.

"We are not accepted in society." The colonel.

"We cannot chaperon her even if anyone invited us anywhere. She is with her mother." Miss Tonks.

"No, wait a bit," said Sir Philip, chewing his thumb. "It's time we had some more publicity. We hold a subscription ball, charge the earth. No one values a cheap affair. Open up the dining-room, the hall and the coffee room. Chalk the floor, get the orchestra, flowers and Despard's cooking. Raise money for our gallant troops. Charge so much per head that we can send a publicity-raising sum to the army and yet pay for everything including wear and tear. Think on't. Patriotic duty to come. That's what they'll think."

"But all that will happen," pointed out Miss Tonks, "is that Arabella will be shut up in her room while her mother attends."

Sir Philip grinned. "Not if you let me handle it."

It was moments like this, thought Lady Fortescue, that one did feel a pang at cheating Sir Philip. It was just as well Miss Tonks had done the bookkeeping so cleverly, for the money paid out to Mr. Davy had to be hidden. In order to even the score, decided Lady Fortescue, the rest of them should force themselves to meet Mrs. Budge's bills until such time as they got rid of her.

"I do not think it will work." Colonel Sandhurst voiced his protest. He was jealous again of Sir Philip now that Sir Philip once more stood high in Lady Fortescue's favour.

"We could set up a committee, Colonel," said the earl. "My name will be on it and that of Miss Carruthers here. I shall praise Lady Carruthers over her daughter's ingenuity and public spirit."

Arabella's eyes were shining. "It would be so wonderful. I could have my first ball gown and ... and ..." Her face fell. "Alas, I do not know how to dance!"

"That is easily rectified," cried Miss Tonks. "Cannot you play the pianoforte a little, Lady Fortescue?"

"Alas, no. I have forgot all I ever learned."

"I can," cried Sir Philip, delighted to be back in favour. "Take your partner, my lord."

A few minutes were spent while they all moved back the furniture and rolled back the carpet. Sir Philip flipped up the tails of his coat and sat down on the piano stool and began to play a jaunty waltz.

The earl put an arm around Arabella's slim waist. She blushed in miserable confusion. The blood seemed to be thumping in her ears, and although it was only a moment before she recovered, it seemed an age before she could hear the music and listen to his instructions. Miss Tonks sat and smiled indulgently. She thought they made such a handsome couple. Arabella gradually grew more confident. After the waltz was over, there were the intricacies of the quadrille to master and then the cotillion. She said she thought she would manage in the country dances, for she had learned those at the servants' parties at home. "You need much more practice," said the earl. "But let us leave that to another evening. Perhaps we should all sit down and discuss arrangements for this ball."

This time Lady Fortescue rang the bell and when her personal servants, John and Betty, answered its summons, she asked them to put the carpet and furniture back. Sir Philip asked for iced champagne and then they settled down to drawing up a guest list... although the invited guests would be expected to pay for the honour of attending the ball.

Mr. Davy was enjoying himself as he had not enjoyed himself for some time. It was glorious to be so well-fed and well-dressed. It was like becoming part of a family and he had to remind himself sternly of what he owed these people, for the temptation to spin out the wooing of Mrs. Budge for as long as possible was very attractive.

The earl was enjoying himself. This was much better fun than attending some boring musicale. Arabella was glowing with beauty. She would no doubt marry very well, unless her mother proved to be mean over her dowry. Perhaps he could persuade Lady Carruthers that she would be better placed to play the young widow were her daughter married and off her hands.

He realized Lady Fortescue was addressing him. "Lord Denby, is it all settled? May we put your name at the head of the committee to give ourselves the necessary ton?"

"By all means," he said politely. "More champagne, Miss Carruthers?"

"Please." Arabella held out her glass. "I now feel I could dance very well."

"Don't become foxed. How is the list going, Sir Philip?"

"We've put down the cream," said Sir Philip. "Now what about the Prince Regent?"

They all stared at him in surprise.

"Why not?" demanded Sir Philip. "He came here for dinner."

"That was because of the reputation of our chef," pointed out the colonel.

"Besides," said Lady Fortescue, "His Majesty is in Brighton."

"Brighton ain't far," said Sir Philip.

"Perhaps I could help there." The earl looked around the room. "I could travel to Brighton and deliver an invitation in person. The prince is very keen on the army."

Everyone, with the exception of Arabella, greeted this idea with enthusiasm. Arabella suddenly could not bear to think of him being absent from the hotel.

"So that's settled," cried Miss Tonks. "How exciting! And what a splendid evening. Quite like old times. I did not know you could play the piano."

"Oh, I have my talents," grinned Sir Philip. He crossed to the piano again and began to play. The champagne flowed. Sir Philip played. Miss Tonks sang in her reedy voice, looking so elated and happy that she achieved a sort of prettiness, and the earl, leaning forward to help himself to more champagne, brushed against Arabella's shoulder and found himself restraining a sudden odd impulse to put an arm about her and give her a hug.

At last Lady Fortescue reminded the poor relations in an amused voice that they were in trade rather than society and had to be up early to go about their duties and so the party broke up.

The earl walked Arabella down to her room door. "I do not know when I have ever enjoyed myself so much as I have done this evening with these odd hoteliers," he said, raising her hand to his lips.

Overcome with confusion, Arabella stammered out a hurried good-night.

She went into her sitting-room and pirouetted around the room, holding the hand he had just kissed against her cheek. She stopped suddenly, aware of being watched, and swung around.

Lady Carruthers was standing in the doorway of her bedroom, staring at her daughter as if she could not believe her eyes. Then she found her voice. "Just what are you doing, miss, wearing my gown? And where have you been?"

"I was talking to Letitia ... to Miss Tonks ... and ... and the others."

"Consorting with tradespeople! And in one of my best gowns."

"But you must hear this, Mama. The hotel is to give a ball and bring me out!"

"Have you run mad? My daughter being brought out in a hotel?"

"But ... but it is to be such a grand ball and—"

Lady Carruthers let out a piercing scream of rage which brought her maid and footman running.

Then she put one hand to her heaving bosom and declaimed, "You will take off that gown and give it to Alice here. You will not go near these hoteliers again. You will stay in your room as punishment and take your meals in your room. Alice, make sure you brush her hair down and leave it down."

"But Lord Denby is to help with the ball."

"Fiddle."

"But it is *true*."

"I will speak to Lord Denby on the morrow, GO TO YOUR ROOM."

Arabella went into her room. The maid prepared her for bed, brushing her hair down her back and, after she was in her night-rail, taking away Lady Carruthers's gown.

Arabella stared dismally at her reflection. She was once more restored in appearance to a school miss. But what was she to do?

***

Sir Philip, who had been sent out on what he considered to be quite an unnecessary errand by Lady Fortescue the next day, returned to the apartment next door to the hotel to find Mrs. Budge out. He was surprised. He was so used to seeing her vast figure either lying in bed, eating chocolates, or sitting in front of the fire, eating cakes.

He felt a slight twinge of relief. It had been such fun last night, all of them happy and very much together again. He had enjoyed Miss Tonks's laughter and the admiration in Lady Fortescue's eyes when he had proposed the ball. But he was an old man, and charms such as Mrs. Budge had to offer had not come his way in years and he was not yet ready to give them up. The fact that he was even contemplating giving them up was an improvement, or so Lady Fortescue would have thought.

Sir Philip went back out into Bond Street and headed for Limmer's Hotel. He had nearly reached it when he saw Mrs. Budge being driven off in a smart curricle by Mr. Davy. He recognized her best bonnet and noticed she was flirting openly. All thoughts of getting rid of her sooner or later fled his mind before a burning wave of jealousy. Davy was the colonel's friend. The colonel should have kept him in check. Be damned to them all and that ball, too. He would punish them all by refusing to help. And what was more, he would propose marriage to Mrs. Budge that very day!

* * *

Mr. Davy found Mrs. Budge an easier companion than he had expected. After an initial bout of nudging and flirting, she had fallen silent and thoughtful and then had become polite and almost like a lady. The fact was that when it came to anything to do with money, Mrs. Budge developed sensitivities she did not normally have. These had not been brought into play much with Sir Philip because it was the coarse and sexual side of Mrs. Budge which pleased him. But she had quickly grasped that Mr. Davy did not relish her openly flirting with him. Out of the corner of her eye, she admired the fine quality of the cloth of his jacket. She remembered that diamond stickpin. Just one jewel like that would set her up for life! She had money in the bank, money which she had never told Sir Philip about, leading him to think instead that she was poor. Her little flat was modest in the extreme, only because she was a compulsive saver of money. Mr. Budge had been her fourth marriage. She had profited from each of her husbands's deaths, retiring into quiet and modest living during each widowhood until she could feather her nest further. And so she let Mr. Davy do most of the talking, and being the actor he was, he was pleased to do so. He invented long and fictional stories about his wealth, about his ships which sailed from the Port of London to China, to the spice islands, to America, and Mrs. Budge listened avidly, editing out the poetic descriptions of countries and fastening on the essentials like ivory, gold, tea, coffee, spices, warehouses, and ships.

***

Lady Fortescue and the colonel were alarmed when an angry Sir Philip, who would not tell them why he was angry, said roundly that he was having nothing to do with the ball for Arabella.

He then went back to the apartment, and when Mrs. Budge returned he asked her to marry him but said nothing about having seen her out with Mr. Davy. Mrs. Budge sighed and placed one chubby hand on her bosom, and to his fury said she would think about it.

He went off to Limmer's again to get drunk.

Meanwhile Lady Fortescue and the colonel had just told Miss Tonks about Sir Philip's refusal to help when Jack, their footman, told them that Lady Carruthers wished to see them.

Lady Fortescue and the colonel went down to her apartment.

"What is this nonsense about holding a ball for Arabella?"

demanded Lady Carruthers. She did not ask either of them to sit.

"We are fond of your daughter and thought it a pleasant idea," said Lady Fortescue mildly.

"The idea does not please me. Arabella will marry all in good time and marry well. She cannot hope to attract the right type of person if she is to be sponsored by tradespeople."

"I would not describe the Earl of Denby as being trade." Lady Fortescue was very stiffly on her stiffs.

"You will find Lord Denby is lending his name to this mad scheme because of his interest in me. It is not necessary. Besides, Arabella is confined to her room with the fever."

"Have you sent for the doctor?" demanded the colonel.

"There is no need. She is used to a quiet life and the air of London does not suit her. Now, I have made myself plain, so that will be all. John"—to her footman—"show these persons out."

"And the lowering thing about being in *trade*," said Lady Fortescue to Miss Tonks sometime later, "is that one has to swallow such insults. Now that Sir Philip has withdrawn his help, there does not seem much point in going on with it."

"Poor Arabella," cried Miss Tonks. "I do not believe she has the fever at all. We must tell Lord Denby."

"Lord Denby left this morning for Brighton," said the colonel, "to nurse the ground, to tell the Prince Regent about our forthcoming ball. He suggested the end of September. Perhaps we should send Jack to Brighton with a message to say it is all off."

"No." Lady Fortescue's black eyes flashed. "We will wait until his return. For if he has met with success, we will use that to coerce Lady Carruthers into allowing Arabella to attend."

***

Arabella paced up and down her room. Her mother had locked her in. She had heard the arrival of Lady Fortescue and Colonel Sandhurst, had heard her mother's reply, and found herself wanting to cry.

Her new friends had a hotel to run. They would have forgotten about her. Arabella did not know that the earl had left so promptly for Brighton.

So as one day dragged into another and he did not come, she thought he, too, had forgotten about her.

CHAPTER FIVE

When I say I know women,
I mean that I don't know them.
Every single woman I ever knew
is a puzzle to me, as, I have no doubt,
she is to herself.
—WILLIAM THACKERAY

The earl returned from Brighton a week later, pleased with his success. The Prince Regent had been in an affable mood and declared that if he was free of engagements, he would find time to attend the ball. Lord Denby knew, however, that the fickle prince could well change his mind before the event; still, he was looking forward to seeing Arabella's eyes light up when he told her the news.

As he walked into the hotel, he met Lady Carruthers, who was dressed to go out.

She fluttered up to him. "Lord Denby! We have missed you."

He bowed. "Your servant, ma'am. And Miss Carruthers?"

She frowned. "The child is poorly, I am afraid. A fever."

"What does the physician say?"

"She has no need of a doctor. It will pass if she is left in peace."

He bowed again and went on past her. Hovering on the landing was Miss Tonks, who gasped, "Is it not terrible?"

"About Miss Carruthers? But I gather it is nothing serious."

"It is my belief," said Miss Tonks earnestly, "that there is nothing up with her. I am convinced she has been locked in her room. Lady Carruthers was most displeased about the idea of the ball and said her daughter was not going to be brought out by tradespeople."

He looked down at her with hauteur. "Does Lady Carruthers know that I have given the project my blessing?"

"Oh, yes. But she does not really believe that and she thinks you are interested in *her*."

"Perhaps we should call on Miss Carruthers and see how she fares?"

"I tried and *tried*, but the outer door is locked, and when the servants are there, they will only say she is not to be disturbed."

"But you have keys to all the doors. You must have!"

"We never use them when the guests are in residence. What if one of them should return and find us there?"

"Miss Tonks, no one seems to have been thinking clearly. The rooms are cleaned, as they are in any home by the servants in the mornings, whether the guests are in residence or not. The chambermaid comes in and draws back the curtains and opens the shutters, takes away the slops and anything that needs to be laundered.

"Oh, *servants*," said Miss Tonks.

"Do not you yourself, as do the others, often act as a servant, Miss Tonks?"

Her face brightened. "Why, yes. When the maids are ill, I myself often see to the rooms. Without loss of dignity, too," she added earnestly, "for no one notices a servant."

"And a footman makes up the fires?" he asked.

"Yes, because although it is quite warm, we pride

ourselves on supplying every luxury, and a fire in the mornings is so *cheering*."

His blue eyes began to dance. "Do Lady Carruthers's servants wake early?"

"I do not think so. There is no reason for them to awake early, as Lady Carruthers does not rise until the early afternoon. She takes her maid and footman with her when she goes out of an evening, and so they often do not get to their own beds until dawn."

"So tomorrow morning," said the earl, "I, as footman, and you as maid, will clean Lady Carruthers's apartment. Bring the keys and we will call on Miss Carruthers."

* * *

At first Lady Fortescue frowned on the idea. Why did the earl not tell Lady Carruthers his momentous news about the Prince Regent? But the earl, although he saw the wisdom of this advice, was perversely determined to play the part of footman so he could see Arabella in person. For he was sure that, even if Lady Carruthers agreed to let Arabella go to the ball, she would keep the girl indoors until then, and he wanted to see her ... just to reassure himself that she was indeed fit and well, he told himself hurriedly.

Sir Philip was present in the office during this discussion. He was in a bad humour. He had just confronted Mr. Davy and told that gentleman to leave Mrs. Budge alone, to which Mr. Davy had replied that as Mrs. Budge was not affianced to Sir Philip, he saw no harm in taking that lady about. Adding to his temper was the fact that his three partners appeared to have accepted the fact that he was going to have nothing to do with the ball and were talking about it as if he weren't even in the room. The knowledge that the Prince Regent might attend was a bitter blow, and yet pride stopped him from saying he had changed his mind. He thought he caught a look of amused contempt in Lady Fortescue's black eyes when she looked at him. He gave a snort of disgust and walked out. He had been in bed with Mrs. Budge one afternoon when Lady Fortescue had walked in. She had seemed not in the slightest put out but had crossed to the bookshelves and extracted a volume, saying that as this sitting-room really belonged to all of them and was only surely a temporary bedroom for Mrs. Budge, she should feel free to come and go "at a reasonable hour of the day." Although Lady Fortescue hailed from a coarser century and did not really belong to the new sentimentality and gentility of this new one, Sir Philip felt her underlying scorn for his liaison with Mrs. Budge. His angry thoughts turned to Mr. Davy. For a friend of the colonel, or rather the son of an old friend, he seemed to spend little time with him, nor, thought Sir Philip with sudden quickening interest, did they reminisce about Mr. Davy's father. He bit his thumb and scowled horribly. Perhaps he should go over to the City and talk to a few friends and ask around the coffee-houses. If this Mr. Davy was as rich and successful as he claimed and owned so many ships and warehouses, then he would be well-known.

He set out on foot, determined to get some exercise. He scuttled along the pavements with his odd crabwise walk. Could it be, he wondered, that this Mr. Davy was some sort of impostor *hired* by his faithless friends to dislodge Mrs. Budge from his side? The more he thought about it, the more feasible it seemed.

Plans on exposing Mr. Davy to Mrs. Budge kept him so amused that he barely noticed the distance he had walked until he reached Ludgate Hill. He made his way up under the shadow of St. Paul's to Child's Coffee-House and pushed

open the door. As his ambling over the years and his scroung-
ing in the days of his poverty had taken him to many taverns
and coffee-houses all over London, he had come to know
people of all classes. He saw a wealthy merchant, Mr. Ezekiel
Brandon, sitting in a corner surrounded by businessmen.
Mr. Brandon was one of the few who had been cheerfully
prepared to buy Sir Philip coffee or wine in the old days. He
looked across the shadowy, low-raftered room and beckoned
Sir Philip, who walked across the oyster-shell-scattered floor.

"Sit down, Sir Philip," said Mr. Brandon. "You look very
fine. I never thought a man like you would turn out to be so
successful in trade."

"Hotel's doing well," said Sir Philip, sitting down in a
chair next to the merchant which had just been vacated by
one of his cronies. "How's business?"

Mr. Brandon discussed trade and stocks and shares while
Sir Philip let his mind wander. He wanted to interrupt, to
brag about the fact that they were to hold a grand ball which
the Prince Regent was to attend but felt frustrated by the
fact that he had sulked himself out of having anything to
do with it. But if this Mr. Davy could be exposed as a fraud,
then he would magnanimously forgive them after they
had grovelled and apologized enough and *then* he would
graciously say he would help them run their ball. He waited
politely until the merchant had finished and then asked
casually, "Heard of a merchant called Davy?"

He waited gleefully for the denial.

Mr. Brandon raised his bushy eyebrows. "Do you mean
Mr. Davy of Pelham, Davy and Briggs?"

Sir Philip's heart sank but he went gamely on. "I believe he's
the son of a friend of Colonel Sandhurst, my partner. Young
chap, well—young to me, in his forties, slim, well set-up."

"Oh, yes, that's our Mr. Davy all right. I'm telling you,

the ships and warehouses that company has, and they started from nothing. I think your Mr. Davy was the brains behind it."

Sir Philip felt very small and crumpled and old. But in memory of past kindnesses, he insisted on treating Mr. Brandon to a bottle of the best burgundy and forced himself to make conversation with Mr. Brandon's friends. He had been so sure that Davy would turn out to be a fraud. How could he, Sir Philip, compete with such riches?

He made his way out and sadly began to walk homewards.

Five minutes after he had left the coffee-house, Mr. Davy of Davy, Pelham and Briggs walked in and was hailed by Mr. Brandon. He was a slim man with a great beaky nose and his head was topped with an old-fashioned wig. "You have just missed a friend," said Mr. Brandon. "Sir Philip Sommerville."

"Never heard of him," said Mr. Davy.

"Said you were a friend of Colonel Sandhurst."

"Never heard of him either."

"Never mind," said Mr. Brandon. "Sir Philip's getting deuced old and probably doesn't know which day it is. Do you know, he asked me about my business and I'll swear he then didn't listen to a word I was saying. So how is your good wife, Mr. Davy, and the children? Well, I trust?"

***

Miss Tonks felt as giggly and conspiratorial as a schoolgirl as she went out to meet the earl the following morning. She was wearing a plain taffeta gown covered with a thin muslin apron. Miss Tonks saw no reason to "dress down" for the part, knowing that such guests who happened to be awake only saw a servant, not what he or she was wearing.

She scratched at the earl's door. He opened it himself.

He was wearing a dark coat and knee breeches covered with a baize apron.

"Jack is on the landing with the bucket for the ashes," whispered Miss Tonks. "To be in character, as our Mr. Davy would say, you rake out the ashes and put them in the bucket and then lay and light the fire. You do not need to polish the grate or anything like that. Jack will come in when we are gone and do the proper work, and Mary, the chambermaid, will do mine. We will work a little in the sitting-room to make sure no one is going to be around to disturb us and then we will unlock Arabella's door."

Miss Tonks fumbled at the ring of keys hanging from her belt until she found the right one. Then she opened the door to Lady Carruthers's apartment. She then had to chide the earl softly on the noise he was making clearing the hearth. "Good servants *never* make a noise." Miss Tonks herself did some perfunctory dusting and cushion-plumping until the fire was set.

She beckoned to the earl and selecting another key, turned it softly in the lock to Arabella's room.

Arabella was not in bed. She was standing by the window looking forlornly down into the street. She turned round as Miss Tonks said, "Arabella," and her eyes lit up.

The earl was furious to see how wan and pale she looked. Her hair was not braided or in ribbons but cascaded to her waist in rippling waves and curls.

"You are not ill, are you, dear?" asked Miss Tonks.

"No, Mama was so annoyed because I put my hair up and wore her gown. I am so bored and weary. Look at the sunshine outside. I feel like a prisoner. *I am a* prisoner."

"You need feel like that no longer," said Miss Tonks eagerly. "See, here is a spare key to your room and one to the outer door. I notice your mama's servants do not leave the key in the door when you are locked in and so you can easily escape anytime you want.

"Come out. Come for a walk with me now," urged the earl. "You look sorely in need of fresh air."

"Mama will not be awake for another few hours," said Arabella, her spirits soaring. "All I need to do is to lock the door behind me." She quickly swung a cloak about her shoulders.

"I need a hat," she suddenly exclaimed. "And my hair is loose. I need ribbons."

"Leave it," said the earl. "We will look like a servant walking his young lady."

Oh, please let Letitia stay behind, Arabella silently prayed. I want him to myself. To her dismay, Miss Tonks gave a little cough and whispered, "You must not go out unchaperoned. I will fetch my bonnet and pelisse."

"I do not think that will be necessary," said the earl with a smile. "No one fashionable will be about at this hour." He took off his baize apron and handed it to Miss Tonks.

"Come along," hissed Arabella, fretting with impatience in case her mother or one of the servants would awake.

She did not relax until she and the earl were outside the hotel and walking down Bond Street towards Piccadilly. There was a brisk breeze and a strand of her flying hair blew across the earl's mouth.

Arabella apologized and hurriedly braided her hair into a pigtail which she fastened with a handkerchief. The earl glanced at this tidying up of all that glorious river of shining hair with regret. He had a sudden vivid picture of what this high-breasted girl would look like naked with her hair tumbling around her body and then he angrily brushed the thought from his mind. She now looked once more like the schoolgirl her mother wished her to appear.

"You have not heard my momentous news," he said.

"I had an audience with the Prince Regent and His Royal Highness graciously said he would try to attend. We must just hope he does not find a more pressing engagement when the time arrives."

Her eyes shone. "But don't you see!" she cried. "Mama must surely be delighted to let me attend the ball. She cannot refuse."

"I considered that. I think Lady Carruthers is so determined to marry again and so determined not to let anything stand in her way that she may find an excuse to keep you in your room. I must think of some plan before I approach her."

"Mama views you in the light of a future husband," said Arabella. "Perhaps ... perhaps if you were to *imply* that as my future papa you would ... you would like to see me at the ball, to see me being brought out, then ... then she might just let me go."

The idea of being a father to this girl made him feel jaded and old, but he had to accept the good sense of what she was saying. But he hesitated. "Perhaps I will put this idea of yours to those odd people at the hotel. They have a great deal of good sense."

They walked into Green Park past the lodge. The sunlight sparkled on the waters of the reservoir. There were no Fashionables about. The hour was too early. "There is a certain freedom in being a servant," commented the earl.

"Only to pretend servants," said Arabella. "Were I a real servant I would hardly ever get out. There is no real freedom for any woman." She gave a little sigh. "I am plotting and planning with you and the others to make my come-out without ever considering the end of it."

"Happily ever after?"

"Only in rare cases, I think. I will need to reward Mama for my clothes and my dowry by marrying well. Provided the gentleman is willing and rich enough, I will not be allowed to refuse his offer. Then I will be led to his bed to bear his children, one after another, until I am too old."

"So young and so cynical," he mocked. "Marriage often means freedom for any lady. She has her own establishment, her own servants. Her husband is often in his club or on the hunting field. She has her own circle of friends ..."

"And takes lovers, or so I have heard," interrupted Arabella.

He looked down at her half-exasperated, half-amused. "Do you never dream of romance, of love?"

"Yes," she said simply, thinking of all her rosy dreams of being married to *him*. "But, you see, I know they are dreams and nothing more. I read novels but I am sensible enough to know that they are only stories."

He felt a stab of pity for her. She should have been surrounded by friends of her own age, giggling about beaux, talking about gowns.

"I am sure you will find happiness," he said. "Does Lady Carruthers attend Lord Fremley's banquet this evening?"

"I believe so. The footman said something about it when he brought in my supper."

"You are not even allowed to go to the hotel dining-room?"

"Not even when I am supposed to be well."

"I have accepted an invitation to the banquet but I can always send my man to say I am unwell. You have the key to your room. Perhaps, after the hotel dinner has been served, we can meet the others in the sitting-room and discuss the ball. Now I have spoken to the prince, it must go ahead."

Her eyes shone at the idea of seeing him again so soon. He took her arm in his and they strolled under the trees and he told her of his home, Bramley Hall.

"Do you have children?" asked Arabella.

"No, no children. My wife was in poor health. I think after this famous ball I shall return to the country. I am not really happy in Town."

Her eyes clouded over. She thought, I would be happy anywhere with him. Why cannot he feel the same for me?

"How is Mr. Davy getting along with Mrs. Budge?" she asked after a short silence.

"That is something we must find out." She glowed at that "we." "He is a charming fellow."

"He sang most beautifully that evening," said Arabella. "If he is that good, then why is he not employed?"

"Unless one is a Kean, a Garrick, or a Siddons, actors can be easily forgotten. The managers have their favourites. Perhaps I will see if there is anything I can do for him. It is a pity he has been hired to flirt with Mrs. Budge."

"Why?"

"Miss Tonks is a lonely lady, I think. Mr. Davy is a courteous gentleman."

"Oh, but Letitia is so unworldly in her way and Mr. Davy would surely find her very tame and dull compared to the actresses he has known."

"He might find her a refreshing change. I must say the hotel fascinates me. I look forward to spending the evening in their sitting-room. Besides, as I said, I would like to consult them before I approach your mother."

She turned her pale face up to the sun and sighed, "Ah, that feels so good."

"Have you no brothers or sisters?" he asked, feeling an odd tug at his heart as he watched her.

"I had two little brothers, twins, but they were carried off in a cholera epidemic. Papa was devoted to the boys. Do you know, much as I mourned their death, I thought perhaps

Papa would turn his attention to me, but he became more addicted to sporting pursuits than ever."

"It must have been a sad blow for your mother."

"I was very young when they died, but yes, I think it was."

"And did she never have much time for you?"

"Not very much, but that is often the case with our kind of people, is it not? Nurses and governesses take the place of parents."

"If I had children, I would cherish them," he said.

"And I. Do you wish only sons?"

"Of course I would like a boy to carry on my name, but girls would be delightful."

"What names would you give them?"

He smiled. "I would call the boy something very simple and English, like William or John." He tugged the braid of her hair. "And I would call the first girl Arabella."

"In memory of another little girl you once knew?" Her voice was sad.

"Well, my chuck, it is hard to think of you as a grown-up lady."

She winced and he added quickly, "But you are very charming and you will break all hearts at the ball."

If only I could break yours, she thought wistfully, but the compliment made her heart begin to sing and sing louder the more she thought about it.

"How dusty the trees look," she said. "They will soon be turning colour, and then winter will come again. I do not like winter in the country, so cold, so dark, so lonely."

"It need not be like that if one has company." And yet he thought of his own lonely winters and had a mental picture of a bright and happy Arabella moving about the rooms of his house, playing the piano, talking about everything and anything. "Tell you what," he said, "I shall invite you and your mama to stay with me for part of the winter. Then we can be lonely together."

She looked up at him cautiously. "I think perhaps you came to Town to find a bride, for they told me you brought a great many clothes with you and yet you do not appear to be a dandy."

"I ordered too many. I had been out of the world for so long that I did not want to appear like a countrified squire. But any bride of mine would accept your presence."

Arabella felt exhausted by her own tumultuous emotions—up one minute, crashing down the next. All her joy at the idea of visiting his home had been dashed by the thought that he might be married by the winter.

"I think I had better return to the hotel," she said in a small voice.

They walked side by side slowly back to the hotel, hardly speaking, Arabella immersed in sad thoughts and the earl feeling he had said something wrong but not wanting much to examine what it was he had said.

***

Sir Philip had his first stand-up, all-out row with Mrs. Mary Budge that afternoon when he caught her getting ready to go out and she said that she was going driving again with Mr. Davy. At first, she had arranged to meet Mr. Davy when she knew that Sir Philip was otherwise engaged, but although greedy, she was lazy by nature and could not be bothered taking too much trouble to cover up her meetings with the actor.

"I forbid you to go," snarled Sir Philip.

"Now, my love," she cooed, "you is often busy with this here hotel, ain't you? So it don't do no harm for me to take the air with Mr. Davy, now does it? You're being a mite unreasonable."

"A pox on you, you fickle ugly old twat," howled Sir Philip, jumping up and down. Her face hardened and her massive bosoms heaved in outrage.

"If you don't watch what you are saying, *old man*, then I'll take my favours elsewhere."

"You do that." Sir Philip's voice was rising to a scream. Mr. Davy, outside the door, listened with glee.

Mrs. Budge crammed her bonnet on her head and turned to leave. But she stopped before she got to the door. Mr. Davy had been charming, but he had suggested no liaison, no commitment. To leave Sir Philip meant leaving free meals and board, not to mention the extras supplied by him. Besides, it would not hurt Mr. Davy to be passed over, just this once. She swung round and held out her chubby arms. "Whose precious is all jealous and upset? Come to Mary, sweetheart." And cajoling and coaxing, she led him to the still-rumpled bed.

Mr. Davy turned quickly away from the door. He went to his own room and sat on the bed. He would have to pitch his suit strongly from now on with Mrs. Budge. She repelled him. At first, she hadn't seemed so bad, but at each meeting, she grew larger and more gross in his eyes. He gave a weary little sigh. If only Sir Philip knew how very lucky he was, to have this life, this hotel, these friends.

***

Arabella did not dare to borrow any of her mother's gowns, but she put her hair up in what she hoped was a fair copy of one of the new Roman styles. Then she softly unlocked her door and, with a feeling of adventure, of release, she scampered up the stairs to the hotel's "staff" sitting-room.

She stood outside the door nervously smoothing down her dress and patting her hair before making her entrance.

The earl was not there, she noticed that immediately, and she sat down next to Miss Tonks, fighting down a stabbing pang of worry that he would not come, that the game had ceased to amuse him. Sir Philip had not arrived. Mr. Davy was explaining that he had not been warm enough in his attentions to Mrs. Budge and he intended to change his tactics on the morrow. The colonel shook his hand and called him a brave man.

"Is Denby coming?" Lady Fortescue asked Arabella.

"He said he would be here."

"There is no allowing for the whims and fancies of young men," remarked Lady Fortescue, echoing Arabella's worries.

At that moment, the door opened and the earl came in. Arabella looked down. She was irrationally cross with him for having frightened her by being late. She was also cross with him for his easy affectionate attitude towards her, the attitude of a man towards a child. She could feel a sort of ugly, mulish, sulky expression settling on her face and tried to think of light and happy things but could not. She was so intensely aware of him, of the smoothness of his tanned skin, of his blue eyes, of the strength of his body, and the slim elegance of his powerful hands. He did not sit down next to her. Now that was not possible as she had Mr. Davy on one side of her and Miss Tonks on the other, but she felt he might have asked one of them to move. A clear, cold part of her brain told her she was being silly in the extreme, but the nasty thoughts would not go away.

She turned to Mr. Davy and smiled up at him in a coquettish way and asked, "Do we really need to wait for Sir Philip? I am sure with your intelligence, Mr. Davy, you can hit on a way of persuading Mama to let me attend this ball."

Man of the world and actor that he was, Mr. Davy

automatically responded to that look by raising her hand to his lips and saying, "You flatter me, miss."

Miss Tonks threw Arabella an agonized look which went unnoticed by her. The earl, who was talking quietly to Lady Fortescue, noticed that flirtatious look of Arabella's and Mr. Davy's kiss and thought with surprise that she really was nothing more than a silly little miss and probably did not merit all the attention she was getting. He gave her a cold look. Arabella promptly began to flirt even harder.

All Miss Tonks's old loneliness crept back. Not only was Arabella being stupid, but Mr. Davy should have known better than to encourage the naïve attentions of a young lady. She was sadly disappointed in Arabella. Mrs. Budley would never have behaved in such a way.

Lady Fortescue, sharper than Miss Tonks, knew exactly why Arabella was behaving so badly. She looked back down the years and remembered behaving just that way because she wanted the one man in the room who was indifferent to her.

Sir Philip came in and looked sourly about him. He sat down in a corner, emitting a "humph."

"Although you are going to have nothing to do with the ball, Sir Philip," said Lady Fortescue, "we will now start the proceedings because of the expense we will need to lay out on the event, an expense, I may add, which we hope to recoup. Now, as we cannot say outright that the Prince Regent will be attending, for he may change his mind, we must nonetheless put the fact about unofficially. Perhaps you would be so good as to help us there, Lord Denby?"

"Gladly," he said in a flat voice, although he was beginning to regret having said he would have anything to do with this ball. Who was Arabella Carruthers anyway? Nothing more than an empty-headed miss.

Sensing his disapproval, Arabella said quickly, "Lord Denby

agreed with me earlier that perhaps if Mama were to think he meant to marry *her*, and that he might be my new father, she would listen to him about allowing me to go to the ball."

"Now that I have had time for reflection, I think that idea a trifle tiresome," said the earl.

Arabella stared at him wide-eyed, a flush beginning to rise up her cheeks.

"Dear me," commented Lady Fortescue acidly. "Now that you have been so good as to get the tacit acceptance of the Prince Regent, Lord Denby, we must go ahead with it, although it seems a great pity to me that as the ball was orig- inally to bring out Miss Carruthers that she should stay *in*."

"I'll see what I can do," said the colonel, glancing at Arabella's distressed face in sympathy.

"It won't work." Arabella's voice was low. "She did not listen to you before."

Sir Philip got up and went and stood in front of the fireplace.

"What a mess you've all been making of a simple problem," he said with contempt. "*I* will get Lady Carruthers to give her permission."

Lady Fortescue gave a little sigh of relief. Arabella looked doubtfully at Sir Philip. He was not wearing his wig and his sparse white hair clung to his pink old man's scalp. He was in his undress, that of slippers and a disgracefully shabby old Oriental dressing-gown. He did not look an imposing figure. Her distress that the earl had seemingly abandoned her cause became too much for her.

She stood up, a small but dignified figure, and said in a small voice, "If you will excuse me, I have the headache."

"I will come with you, Arabella." Miss Tonks rose to her feet as well.

"No, no," she said rapidly, and almost ran from the room.

Lady Fortescue briskly got down to business. The invitations would be written out and sent the following day. The preliminary invitations would be in the form of letters. Only those who paid up the large sum demanded would receive that magic gilt-edged card of definite invitation.

Without asking the earl again for his permission, she decided to phrase the initial onslaught as being sponsored by the Earl of Denby, Lady Fortescue, Colonel Sandhurst, Sir Philip Sommerville and Miss Tonks. The price of attendance would be fifty guineas per head, profits to go to the army.

The earl listened bemused as these aristocrats toted up sums and subtracted others, discussed menus and decorations with efficient ease. The business finally having been settled, Lady Fortescue rang the bell and ordered wine and cakes.

But Sir Philip, now that he felt he was restored to favour, concentrated his attention on his rival who, that evening, had his hair powdered.

"We must be sure to make a profit from this ball," said Sir Philip, glaring at Mr. Davy's head, "for it is not as if *all* of us are rich enough to powder our heads."

Hair powder was first taxed in 1786, when a duty of a penny on all powders sold at under two shillings a pound was imposed, with higher rates for the more expensive varieties. Then, from 1795, all persons powdering their hair were required to take out an annual licence costing a guinea. There were special terms for fathers with more than two unmarried daughters, and for servants; but those who only wore powder occasionally complained that they were being as highly rated as those who were in constant practice of powdering. This tax, it is said, hit the hairdressers hard: even so, in its first year it yielded £210,136. A number of people were prosecuted for failing to possess licences. Among them was Lady Bessborough, who was examined by the Middlesex justices for some

three hours in March of 1798. A snooping informer read a
long list of occasions on which she and others of her household had used hair powder; and her ladyship added to the list
by confessing to have worn powder when she went to divine
services at St. Paul's. Since she had, in fact, given her servant
the money for taking out her licence, which he had not done,
her fine was reduced from £240 to £60. Over 46,000 still paid
the duty in 1812: thereafter the numbers gradually decreased.
The distress caused by poor harvests and the war caused
certain ladies to say they left off wearing hair powder out of
patriotism. But as only poor-quality hair powder contained a
small proportion of flour, the better variety being mostly of
talc, it was assumed they just did not want to pay the tax.

Mr. Davy smiled sweetly on Sir Philip and refused to
rise to the old man's gibe. Although this annoyed Sir Philip
greatly because he liked to think of himself as a Machiavel-
lian type of person who never let his temper get the better
of him, he had not quite worked out in his mind that his
current jealousy of Mr. Davy was beginning to spring not
from Mr. Davy's courtship of Mrs. Mary Budge but because
of the man's looks and wealth and younger years. Also, that
silly sheep of a woman, Miss Tonks, kept gazing on this Mr.
Davy with adoring eyes. Sir Philip had just made love to Mrs.
Budge, or rather what usually passed for making love among
the gentlemen of the Regency; that is, the quickest, shortest
intercourse possible. The lady's feelings were never taken
into account. Ladies were not supposed to have passions,
even ladies such as Mrs. Budge. Only tarts enjoyed it. So
the idea of actually "making love" to Mrs. Budge had never
entered the old man's head any more than it had entered it
in the affairs of his youth. So with his lusts recently satisfied,
Sir Philip felt that Mr. Davy no longer stood a chance with
the widow and so he hated him for himself alone.

"I like a man with his hair powdered," simpered Miss Tonks.

"Oh, what do you know about men, you old spinster?" jeered Sir Philip.

Miss Tonks gazed on Sir Philip's pink scalp. "More than you know about hair, you old fool," she said. "Doesn't your scalp get *cold* lying about *bare* like that?"

"Children, children," mocked Lady Fortescue. "Let us have harmony. Sir Philip, now that my Lord Denby has backed down, I am delighted and pleased that you have decided to tackle Lady Carruthers."

"Yes, indeed," seconded the colonel gruffly. "No one can handle a difficult situation like you, Philip."

The rare use of his first name, the rare praise from a man he often regarded as his rival made Sir Philip glow. His mercurial spirits rose. He patted Miss Tonks's hand and said, "We are always quarrelling, are we not? But we must not quarrel, not when you are looking so pretty."

And so for the second time in her life, she had been called pretty, and Miss Tonks glowed with happiness.

The earl felt shut out from all the "family" bonhomie. They had each in their way silently damned him for refusing to help Arabella.

He rose and made his farewells to the company and was well aware that all were relieved to see him go.

Feeling strangely diminished, he made his way downstairs. He hesitated outside the door of Lady Carruthers's apartment and then knocked loudly on it, knowing that Arabella could surely hear him, even from her bedroom. He waited and waited, but no Arabella came to answer the door.

But Arabella, with the pillows over her head and crying into the sheet, had not heard him.

CHAPTER SIX

The devil, depend upon it,
can sometimes do a
very gentlemanly thing.
—ROBERT LOUIS STEVENSON

*A*rabella awoke with a feeling that her young life was at an end. She had behaved in a way to give the earl a disgust of her. And in the clear light of day in a locked hotel bedroom, she had little hope that Sir Philip would achieve what Lady Fortescue and Colonel Sandhurst had failed to do. But she could not help hoping that Sir Philip would clean himself up a bit for the audience with her mother and not appear in his undress and wearing his second-best teeth, which were of wood.

In the afternoon, she heard her mother and servants go out. She sat moodily in a chair by the window, too depressed to take out that precious key and allow herself some freedom.

Then she heard an urgent scratching at the door and Miss Tonks's voice whispering, "Let me in, Arabella."

Arabella went and unlocked the door.

"He doesn't care a rap for me," she said passionately.

Miss Tonks looked sympathetic but she said, "You did bring it on yourself, Arabella. What prompted you to flirt in that bold way with Mr. Davy?"

"He did not sit next to me," muttered Arabella.

"But how could he, my dear? You already had Mr. Davy on one side and me on the other."

"I suppose that is that." Arabella shrugged, preferring not to answer the question. "Mama will never agree to my going to that ball anyway."

"That is why I am come. Now you are to do exactly as Sir Philip orders. I know it will sound most odd, but he has never failed us yet."

A look of hope gleamed in Arabella's large eyes.

"What must I do?"

"You must brush down your hair and be sure to wear a white dress. You must stand by your window and look down into Bond Street and you must look wistful. You are occasionally to dab at your eyes with a handkerchief."

"What on earth is that man about?"

"I know it sounds mad. It does so to me," said Miss Tonks earnestly. "But please do it. I have brought the first volume of the latest novel from the circulating library and I will read to you to pass the time."

"It seems so silly ..."

"Please do as he says."

Arabella began to laugh. "Very well. Do you think he wants me to look like the princess in the ivory tower so as to melt Mama's heart?"

"Possibly. Now sit down at the toilet-table and I will help to brush your hair."

**

To Sir Philip's delight, the coffee room at Limmer's was full of bucks and Corinthians, Fops, and Pinks of the Fancy. He ordered wine, sat down at a table, and heaved a great theatrical sigh.

Mr. Fotheringay and Mr. Dessel stopped at his table and stared down. "What's up, Sommerville?" drawled Mr. Fotheringay. "Got the blue devils?"

"It's a tragedy," said Sir Philip, shaking his head. "Breaks my heart."

"You ain't got a heart to break," commented Mr. Dessel with a loud guffaw. "I say." He addressed the room at large. "Sommerville has had his heart broken."

The men lounged up to the table, grinning, picking their teeth, flicking their snuff-boxes and waving their handkerchiefs. Amused voices called on Sir Philip to elaborate.

"It's like something out of a Haymarket tragedy," said Sir Philip, privately and gleefully noticing that he now had a large audience. "Lady Carruthers is resident at my hotel. She has a beautiful daughter."

Cries of "You old rake!"

Sir Philip held up his small white hands for silence. "Silence, gentlemen. Arabella Carruthers is only nineteen. She is so beautiful, Lady Carruthers is frightened that if she exposes this treasure to the world, then no one will look at *her*."

"Painted trollop," commented Mr. Fotheringay. "Wouldn't look at her anyway."

"Such is her great vanity, *she* don't know that. So she keeps this diamond of the first water locked up day and night in a hotel bedroom. So me and my partners decided on a plan to bring the girl out ourselves. We are holding a grand subscription ball—tickets fifty guineas, only the cream invited—and the Prince Regent is to attend. But has this melted Lady Carruthers's flinty heart? Not a bit of it."

"You're bamming us," jeered Mr. Dessel.

"Go along Bond Street," urged Sir Philip, "and stand opposite the hotel and look up. She stands there by the window, day in and day out."

There were cries to the effect that they would all go and have a look at Sir Philip's charmer.

Gleefully, Sir Philip followed the crowd of men along Bond Street. He looked up at the hotel windows and heaved a sigh of relief.

Arabella could be quite clearly seen. Her shining hair fell about her shoulders, and even from the distance of across the road, it could be seen that her beautiful face was sad and wistful.

Most of the men who watched in startled silence were brutal products of an age of hard drinking, wenching and fighting. But this was also the age of sentimentality when men prided themselves on the soft hearts that so few of them really had. "It is so tragic," cried Mr. Dessel and began to sob. Mr. Fotheringay, not to be outdone, took out a cambric handkerchief the size of a bed sheet and blew his nose loudly.

More gentlemen stopped and joined the crowd. It was all very exciting to the Bond Street loungers, better than a play.

"Miss Tonks, it is very embarrassing," said Arabella over her shoulder. "All these men are staring up at me and some of them are crying."

"Is Sir Philip among them?"

"Yes, he keeps stopping more gentlemen and pointing up at me."

"Oh, I know what he is doing," cried Miss Tonks. "Here is a pretty little handkerchief. Now you must slowly raise it to your eyes and dab them."

"How long do I have to do this?"

"I should think until your mama returns."

* * *

Lady Carruthers was feeling somewhat pleased with herself. She had made several calls and she knew a new dinner-gown would be waiting for her at the hotel. She had heard of the earl's return and planned to dazzle him in the dining-room that evening. She was just reflecting that she had been too hard on Arabella—she would send the girl back to the country—when her carriage arrived outside the Poor Relation. It was an open carriage, so the men on the other side of the road had a good view of her, as did Arabella, who cried to Miss Tonks, "Here's Mama."

Miss Tonks ruthlessly pulled her away from the window, and a loud cry of "Shame!" went up from the watchers.

"Here is Lady Carruthers now," said Sir Philip. "Boo!"

Bewildered, Lady Carruthers descended from the carriage and stared across the road at the angry faces, heard the loud hisses and boos, and then turned and ran into the hotel.

By the time she reached her apartment, Miss Tonks had gone and Arabella was once more locked in her room.

Lady Carruthers succumbed to a strong fit of hysterics while her maid tried to soothe her. At the end of half an hour, she relapsed into a morose silence.

"Sir Philip Sommerville," announced her footman from the doorway.

"We are not at home," said Lady Carruthers despite the fact that Sir Philip was standing in the open doorway and could hear every word.

Unfazed, Sir Philip walked in, flipped up his coat-tails and sat down.

"This is an outrage," cried Lady Carruthers.

"I come to help you, my lady," said Sir Philip, not budging an inch. "Do you not want to know why all the gentlemen in Bond Street were hissing you and booing you?"

"The behaviour of louts does not concern me."

"They were not louts, and by tonight," pursued Sir Philip, "the story will be all over London."

She looked at him uneasily. "What story?" she asked.

"How you keep your beautiful daughter locked in her room, how you never take her anywhere, how you dress her in a child's clothes ... need I go on?"

"Who has been spreading such scurrilous lies?"

"Hotel servants will talk. We all know Miss Carruthers is not ill, as you claim."

"Pray leave. You are impertinent."

He shook his head sadly. "You could have had my help. Now how are you to face the world when you next go out? No more cards will arrive for you and you will be as isolated as your daughter. Furthermore, the Prince Regent is to attend our ball. Unless you repair your reputation and do it quickly, then, for the sake of the good name of our hotel, we cannot invite you, even though the main purpose of the ball was to bring your daughter out."

Lady Carruthers went pale under her rouge. She could think of no worse fate than being socially ostracized. The full impact of his words finally sank in.

"What am I to do?" she asked weakly.

"You have an engagement for this evening?"

"Yes. The Macleans's rout."

"Then take your daughter, dress her well, put her hair up, show every evidence of being the doting mother and maintain the fiction that she has just got over an illness."

Arabella, listening on the other side of the door, pressed her ear harder against the panels.

And then she heard her mother say with an obvious effort, "Very well. I will follow your advice."

Sir Philip's heart softened as it always did when he got his own way. He stood up. "You know," he said, putting his head on one side and surveying her, "you'd be a fine figure of a woman if you dressed your age."

***

The earl was not in the dining-room and so missed the splendid sight of Miss Arabella Carruthers in a dainty white gown ornamented with silk rose-buds and with a coronet of roses in her shining hair. Arabella felt quite cast down. She had been so excited at the thought of seeing him.

But it was exciting later to be out in the wicked London streets joining all the other Fashionables who were going out for the evening. Arabella had never been to a rout. For a brief while she forgot about the earl and her yearnings for him and looked forward to her first London social engagement.

A Regency rout was not an elegant affair. The purpose of it was to invite as many people as possible and cram as many people as possible into one house. Success was ensured if it were called "a sad crush." Their carriage lined up with the other carriages waiting to draw up outside the Macleans's house. Coachmen fought with each other for positions, carriages inched forward; outside, the rain began to fall, sad, steady rain which drummed on the carriage roof.

Arabella began to fret that the party would be over by the time they arrived, but when the carriage finally drew up at the house, Arabella, looking out, saw the rooms filled with guests, for all the curtains were drawn back, as they always were at a rout.

Holding her skirts high so that they would not be soiled by the wet pavement, Arabella scurried indoors beside her mother. They left their cloaks in an ante-room and then joined the long queue on the staircase who were waiting to go above-stairs to pay their respects to the hostess. People trying to get up shoved and jostled and people trying to get down shoved and jostled. One lady trying to get down was pushed from behind and fell forward and the people in front of her tumbled forward also, down into the hall like so many dominoes. One lady lay on the hall floor with her skirts above her head, exposing her bare bottom. The men in front and behind Arabella caused more fuss by trying to get a better view.

The air was suffocatingly warm and redolent of sweat, unwashed bodies, and all the latest scents on the market—Suave, Sans Pareille, Vento's Italian Water, Cannes and Miss in her Teens. There was also a strong smell of musk from the pastilles that a great number sucked to counteract the smell from their rotting teeth.

Gradually Arabella became used to being openly stared at. By the time they reached the drawing-room, she was feeling crumpled and jaded. Lord and Lady Maclean were standing by the fireplace.

"And this is your daughter," cried Lady Maclean. "Beautiful. Quite beautiful. Such tales we have heard," she added archly. "We heard you were a prisoner."

"I had a touch of the fever and had to be confined to my room," said Arabella to her mother's infinite relief.

"You will break hearts," said Lord Maclean.

Arabella and Lady Carruthers moved away to talk to the other guests before beginning the battle downwards again. They were immediately surrounded by gentlemen. Arabella, at first startled and then gratified by all the compliments and attention, began to glow. Lady Carruthers was experiencing the novelty of being the centre of a group of adoring courtiers, and although their interest was obviously not in her, it was miles better than being isolated. For the first time she realized properly that her daughter was first-class bait. While Arabella chatted easily, maintaining the fiction that she had been ill, her eyes occasionally glanced this way and that, looking for the tall figure of the earl. But there was no flash of blue eyes or glint of guinea gold hair. Beginning to feel a little cast down again, she accepted an invitation from Mr. Fotheringay to go driving in the Park the following afternoon.

They finally said their goodbyes and joined the crowd going down the stairs, where Arabella discovered the other horror of a London rout, which was standing on the doorstep for half an hour waiting for the carriage to be brought round.

"That went very well," said Lady Carruthers graciously. "I am glad now that I decided to take you about."

"This ball," said Arabella cautiously, "that is to be held in the hotel ...?"

Lady Carruthers manufactured a yawn and affected boredom. "Oh, I suppose we must attend." And a happy Arabella was diplomatically prepared to leave it at that.

"Faith, an early night at last," said Lady Carruthers when they arrived at the hotel. "It is only midnight. But a good night's sleep will refresh me. We must order a wardrobe for you. It is a pity I gave you permission to go driving with young Fortheringay, for you will need fittings. Fotheringay is all very well, but you can do better."

Arabella waited impatiently until her mother had retired for the night. Would there be anyone above-stairs in the sitting-room? Would the earl be there?

At last unable to wait any longer, she scampered up the stairs, knocked at the sitting-room door and opened it. The room was dark and shadowy, lit only by the red gleam from the dying fire.

She was reluctant to leave, reluctant to believe that the evening was over.

She moved into the room, the train of her dress whispering over the floor. She thrust a taper between the bars of the grate and lit the candles on the mantelpiece and stared at her wavering reflection in the glass. A drowned face stared back at her from the old mirror.

She gave a little sigh and then went to the piano. Holding the taper, she lit the candles in their brass brackets, then sat down and began to play.

* * *

The earl had gone to the rout after Arabella had left and heard on all sides about London's newest beauty. Mr. Fotheringay was bragging loudly that he had stolen a march on them all. So the miracle had happened. The awful Sir Philip had said he would get Arabella out and it seemed he had succeeded. The earl did not stay long. He had walked, despite the rain, being too countrified to submit to fashion and arrive in a carriage. There had been many eligible misses at the rout and yet he had not spent much time with any of them. He would need to start searching in earnest for a wife. But the evening had been dull. If he had gone to that odd hotel sitting-room, perhaps he might have been able to dance with Arabella ... But Arabella was now out and Arabella would be flirting and dancing with every man in London. Immersed in his thoughts, he took a short cut down a dark alley leading through to Bond Street and almost did not see the two thugs who were set to waylay him until it was almost too late. As it was, he came to his senses and drew his sword-stick. He fenced and feinted on the slippery cobbles, keeping his back to a wall, avoiding the blows from the cudgel of one and making sure the other had no opportunity to creep round behind him.

At last he thrust the blade into one man's arm and swung round looking for the other. But the wounded man's companion had fled. The earl walked on. This was London. Full of footpads and smells and posturers and silly little misses.

He marched into the hotel and up to his apartment where his man relieved him of his wet hat and greatcoat. "And clean my sword, Gustav," said the earl. "There is blood on it."

"Have we been attacked, my lord?"

"Yes, an everyday occurrence. No, I am not yet ready for bed."

He hesitated in the middle of his sitting-room. He wondered if the poor relations were still awake. It would be fun to find out how Sir Philip had achieved the miracle, even though the thought that he himself had refused to help Arabella still made him feel shabby.

He left his apartment and climbed the stairs, hearing, with a lightening of the heart, the jaunty strains of a waltz.

He looked in at the sitting-room door. Arabella was playing the piano. He crossed the room quietly and stood beside her. She glanced up and her fingers stumbled into silence on the keys.

"Where is everyone?" he asked.

"Gone to bed a long time ago, I think," she said. "Oh, such wonderful news. I have been to a rout this evening."

"So I understand. I arrived at the Macleans's after you had gone. Come and sit down in front of the fire and tell me how Sir Philip achieved such success."

She sat down on the sofa next to him, hardly able to believe that he was here with her and seeing her in all her finery. "It is vastly amusing, now I think about it," said

Arabella. "After Mama had left this afternoon, Sir Philip sent Letitia, Miss Tonks, with instructions that I was to brush my hair down and wear a white dress and stand by the window and look down into the street. This I did. Then I saw a large group of men, all looking up. Sir Philip was there among them. When Mama arrived, they all began to boo and hiss. Then Sir Philip called on Mama and said the story was about Town that she had been keeping me confined and that unless she did something about it, her reputation would be ruined. He even said"—Arabella stifled a giggle—"that if she did not repair her reputation, then she could not attend the ball, as they had the good name of the hotel to think of. So I was put into one of Mama's very best gowns, as you can see, and taken to the rout.

"It was not what I expected. There were a great number of men who said very pretty things to me, and a Mr. Fotheringay is to take me driving tomorrow. But it was such a crush, and no cards or music or dancing or refreshments, only push and shove to get in and push and shove to get out. Why does one have to go to these affairs?"

"To see and be seen," said the earl. "And why is Mr. Fotheringay, he of the large nose and oily hair, favoured above all others?"

"He was the first to ask me, don't you see? So many invitations and compliments, I was quite bewildered."

"I am sure you will be engaged to be married before I," he said easily.

"Have you ... have you met anyone?"

"No, not yet. But I shall. London is thin of company, but there is enough."

"It is all so sordid," muttered Arabella, tracing the pattern in the worn Persian rug with one little kid slipper. "Why cannot people fall in love like they do in books?"

"Oh, romances."

"Not only romances, but in Shakespeare and in other great works of literature."

He smiled into her eyes. "So you believe in love?"

She looked back at him defiantly, tilting up her chin. "Of course."

Her lips were very soft and pink. He leaned forward and kissed her gently on the mouth. "Then I hope you find your heart's desire," he said. A lump rose in her throat. She got quickly to her feet. "The hour is late, my lord," she said. She dropped a low curtsy. "Your servant, my lord."

And then she quickly left the room. He could still smell her light perfume. He could feel her lips. He should not have kissed her. But she was worth more than a fellow like Fotheringay!

***

Arabella herself came to that conclusion the following day. Mr. Fotheringay drawled, Mr. Fotheringay talked about horseflesh and hunting, Mr. Fotheringay talked endlessly about his pet subject, which was Mr. Fotheringay, so that by the time he returned Arabella to the hotel, she was feeling quite desperate, particularly when her mother greeted her with a pleased smile and said that young Fotheringay would do very well after all and she had not expected to have her daughter off her hands so soon. In order to get rid of this beautiful daughter, attractive bait though she was, Lady Carruthers had obviously made up her mind that life would be more comfortable with Arabella married.

So in the dining-room that evening, it was the mother who flirted with the earl when he stopped at their table and the daughter who studied her plate of soup as if she had never seen anything quite so interesting in her life and barely looked up.

"Such a handsome man," sighed Lady Carruthers. "And did you mark the way he looked at me? Would you not like such a handsome father, my dear?"

"Yes, Mama," said Arabella, thinking privately that to be jealous of one's own mother must really be plumbing the depths of moral depravity.

Lady Carruthers was going to the play with a Mrs. Banks, an old friend. Arabella pleaded a headache. She felt wretched, and the only person she could think of who might be able to help her was the awful Sir Philip.

***

Neither Mrs. Budge nor Mr. Davy were in the sitting-room that night after dinner. Sir Philip was in a foul mood because Mrs. Budge had said she was going to sleep, but when he had tried the door of her room, he had found it locked, and now, with the absence of Mr. Davy, he feared that the man was either in there with her or out somewhere with her and he felt sorely betrayed.

Miss Tonks, too, was silent and depressed. But Arabella was determined to get help, so after sitting next to Sir Philip and thanking him very prettily for having helped her, she said, "I would beg you to help me again, sir, for you are the only person I can turn to."

Sir Philip's mood immediately lightened. He loved praise, and praise from such a pretty young thing was doubly welcome. He patted her hand and said, "What is the problem? I will see what I can do."

"It is Lord Denby, as usual," said Arabella. "Thanks to

you, Mama took me out to the Macleans's rout, but he did not arrive until after I had left."

"Routs aren't the place for courting," put in Lady Fortescue. "Never could stand them. As crowded as Bartholomew Fair, and every bit as noisy."

"But a great many men paid me compliments," went on Arabella, "and a Mr. Fotheringay invited me to go driving with him this afternoon, which I did."

"Fotheringay's a loose fish," said Sir Philip, picking at his false teeth with a goose-quill.

"Exactly," cried Arabella. "But Mama wants me off her hands and thinks he would do very well. But there is worse to come."

The colonel smiled on her indulgently. "Go on."

"After Mama had gone to bed I came up here, looking for company, but you had all gone to bed, so I began to play the piano. Lord Denby came in. He said he had heard about Sir Philip's success and wanted to know how he had done it and so I told him. He said I would be engaged before he was and laughed at me because I said I believed in love. Then he kissed me."

"He should not have done that, Arabella," exclaimed Miss Tonks. "Not the *thing* at all. But surely that means he has some tender feelings for you."

"But that is the problem! It was a casual, indifferent embrace, the kind an uncle will give to a niece." Arabella clutched Sir Philip's coat-sleeve. "You *must* help me. You must! Please! You must do something to make him look on me as a real woman."

"Now, then," admonished Lady Fortescue, "I cannot see what Sir Philip can possibly do."

"Ho, you can't, can you?" demanded Sir Philip. "Lay you a wager I can."

Lady Fortescue's black eyes sparkled. "Very well, Sir Philip. If you succeed in bringing about a match between Miss Carruthers and Lord Denby, we will pay Mrs. Budge's bills."

The colonel looked alarmed. "I say, that's not fair." He meant that as they had been going to pay Mrs. Budge's bills to make up for financing Mr. Davy trying to get rid of her, it was hardly fair that this should be the subject of a wager.

"Never mind him," said Sir Philip gleefully. He turned to Arabella. "Now I'll bet you want me to fix up something noble for you to do so that Denby can see you are a mature woman of worth?"

Arabella clasped her hands. "Oh, that is it exactly!"

He shook his head. "Wrong! Gentlemen don't like clever ladies. Need to bring out the knight errant in him. Need him to save you from folly."

"What folly?" Lady Fortescue's voice held a warning note.

"Shan't tell you," said Sir Philip gleefully. "I'll tell Miss Carruthers here when I'm good and ready!"

**

Arabella began to think that Sir Philip had forgotten about her. In the week that followed, she went everywhere with her mother and drove out in the afternoons with various gentlemen and wondered what the earl was doing and if he had found someone. But a week to the day she had spoken to Sir Philip, Miss Tonks called on her in the morning and said Sir Philip wanted to see her in the office. "But do be careful, Arabella," said Miss Tonks. "Sir Philip can come up with some very wild schemes indeed."

When they both entered the office, Sir Philip said brutally to Miss Tonks, "Off with you, sheep-face."

"Why are you so horrible to Letitia?" demanded Arabella.

"Cos she's horrid to me that's why. Don't worry about Miss Tonks. Lots of bottom there. Shot a highwayman stone-dead. Tell you that, hey?"

"Yes, she did."

"Don't let's bother about it. Here's what you're to do. There's a costume ball at the Pantheon tonight. Full of disreputable people. You'll be going as my partner. I've got you a costume... in the box over there. Now you just do as I say and everything'll come right and tight. After tonight, he won't be able to look at you and see anything but a woman. Tell your mama you've got the megrims and leave the rest to me. Take the costume and hide it in your room where she can't find it, or that maid of hers, for that matter. Do you trust me?"

"Yes, I do," said Arabella, fighting down a pang of uneasiness.

"Right. Don't breathe a word of where you are going to Miss Tonks or any of the others. Promise?"

"Yes, I promise," said Arabella.

She passed the rest of the day in such a high state of excitement that her mother, who had some residue of maternal feeling, became concerned over her daughter's flushed cheeks and readily agreed that a quiet evening in bed would be just the thing to restore Arabella to good health.

Arabella waited until Lady Carruthers had left and then slid the box containing her costume out from under the bed. She drew it out and held it up and looked at it doubtfully. There seemed to be very little of it. A label on the box said simply "Venus."

There were pink tights to go with it. The costume itself was of the finest white muslin, and there was a pretty head-dress of gold vine leaves, and gold vine leaves adorned the high waist.

Arabella undressed and put the flimsy costume on. The drapery of the white gown felt quite reassuringly substantial. She peered in the glass wishing she had a full-length mirror. There was one in her mother's bedroom, but her mother locked her bedroom door as a security precaution when she went out in the evening. Arabella was still young enough and innocent enough to believe that older people knew best, and Sir Philip was so very old. She put a long fur-lined cloak about her, sat down and nervously waited for Sir Philip to call for her.

***

The earl was playing cards in his club when a note in the shape of a cocked hat was handed to him. "My lord," he read, "I am at my wits' end. I understand our Miss Carruthers has crept out to go to a ball at the Pantheon in an indecent costume. I am an old man and beg your help in rescuing her from a disastrous evening. Your Humble and Obedient Servant, Sommerville."

The earl threw down his cards, crumpled the note and stuffed it in his pocket. He glanced at the clock. Midnight! How long had that innocent been there, and to what insult might she have been exposed?

***

"I hope he hurries up," said Sir Philip anxiously. "I'm not strong enough for this."

He was uneasily aware that Arabella was creating a sensation. In the diaphanous gown over the pink tights and pink silk bodice, she looked half-naked and very desirable. He felt guilty. He had not thought she would look quite so seductive. Various young men had tried to crash into the box and he had sent them about their business. But there had been heavy drinking going on. And then he saw a party of bloods in various historical costumes eyeing the box and whispering together.

Then they began to march purposefully towards it. "Oh, Lord, here it comes," moaned Sir Philip. "Why didn't I bring my gun?"

"What is happening?" asked Arabella. She stood up to get a better look.

And that is how the horrified earl saw her. She looked magnificent, she looked half-naked, she looked as if she had come to be raped, and that, thought the earl, noticing the men approaching the box, was exactly what was going to happen to her.

He thrust his way across the floor, through the sweating, leering costumed dancers, noticing as he did so that most of the women were prostitutes.

"Denby, thank God," said Sir Philip, seeing the earl's approach. "Now you are to say you wanted a bit of fun and it was all your idea, mind?"

Just as the men reached the door at the back of the box, the earl vaulted over the front. He seized Arabella round the waist and swung her over the side onto the ballroom floor, jumped after her, picked her up in his arms and thrust his way forcefully back through the crowd, who laughed and cheered.

"My cloak," wailed Arabella as he carried her straight outside and tumbled her into his carriage.

"Drive on," shouted the earl to his coachman. He jumped in after her and slammed the door.

"Not a word," he said, "until I have you safely back."

In vain did Arabella protest that she did not think it would be quite so dreadful; he only repeated, "Not a word."

She felt it had all gone dreadfully wrong. She should not

have listened to Sir Philip. She fought down the tears. She would not cry. But how was she to explain why she had gone to a place like that? If she was not to mention Sir Philip's part in it, and she could not or the old man might tell the earl how she had appealed to him for help, how could she explain *why* she had gone?

He took off his cloak and said harshly, "Put that round you."

When they arrived at the hotel, he said, "Come with me. Thank goodness all the guests are obviously still out."

Arabella hesitated outside his apartment. "I cannot go in there," she pleaded.

"I am not going to rape you, which is more than I can say for the men at the ball. In with you. Ah, Gustav, take yourself off."

"Very good, my lord," said the wooden-faced servant.

"Wait there," commanded the earl after the servant had gone. He went into his bedroom and returned carrying a long mirror on a stand. "Now take off that cloak," he ordered roughly, "and look at yourself."

Arabella did as she was bid and stared in horror at her reflection. Her *legs*, those members which were never even mentioned in polite conversation, were clearly visible through the thin muslin of her gown, as were her nipples. She gave a little shriek and seized up the cloak again and wrapped it around her.

"Exactly," said the earl with grim satisfaction. "I did not think you were fully aware of just how dangerously disgraceful that costume is."

"I d-did n-not know," wailed Arabella, her face red with shame.

"Sit down," he commanded, "and tell me what possessed you."

Damning Sir Philip in her heart but determined to keep her promise to him, Arabella tugged the cloak closer about her shoulders and said, "I have, my lord, led a very isolated life, a very prim and respectable life. I wanted to see the *real* London and ... and I had never been to a costume ball. Someone in the street sold me a ticket. I am so sorry I caused you and Sir Philip so much trouble."

"Promise me you will never do such a thing again."

"I promise," said Arabella in a low voice.

"Then you had better return to your room."

"I shall return your cloak tomorrow." Arabella looked up at him pleadingly. "Do not be angry with me."

He was suddenly sharply aware of that magnificent half-naked body under the cloak, of her perfume, of the glory of her hair, and his face softened. "Go along with you," he said quietly, "before I forget myself. I shall never be able to think of you as a schoolgirl again."

And it was that sentence which came back to Arabella during a night of fitful sleep, that sentence which suddenly warmed her, that sentence which showed her at last that the wicked and ruthless Sir Philip Sommerville had known what he was doing.

The following day, the earl persuaded himself it would be a good idea to take young Arabella out for a drive and lecture her further on her folly. But a delighted Lady Carruthers seemed to think the invitation was for her, with Arabella added as an afterthought, and so they drove off in his curricle, with Arabella sitting between the earl and her mother.

As the carriage rounded a corner, he could feel Arabella's hip against his own and once more he had a vision of her in that wretched costume. She needed someone to look after her!

CHAPTER SEVEN

*Open and obvious
devotion from any sort
of man is always pleasant
to any sort of woman.*
−RUDYARD KIPLING

*J*t was when an official acceptance from the Prince
Regent arrived that the Poor Relation Hotel was
thrown into more of a turmoil than it had ever been
before in its chequered career.

Not one of them, and that included the earl, had ever
supposed that the prince would really attend. Sir Philip sent
a notice of the fact to the newspapers, and acceptances and
money poured in by post and by hand. Aristocrats were even
travelling up from their country estates for the big event.

But with the strain of all the preparations, tempers
ran higher than they had ever done before, and even the
colonel and Lady Fortescue squabbled over trifles. Sir
Philip tried to advise the head chef, Despard, on the menu
for the supper and had a pot thrown at his head. Only
the guests did not mind the uproar or that they now had
to take their meals in their rooms, as downstairs—that is,
dining-room, hall and coffee room—were stripped bare
preparatory to turning the whole space into a ballroom,

for to be a guest in the hotel automatically meant securing a prized invitation.

Only Mrs. Budge ate her way placidly through the days. Mr. Davy had found the reason that she would not commit herself to him was that she was determined to attend the ball, and she said that if she left Sir Philip, he would make sure her invitation was torn up. So Mr. Davy extracted a promise from the widow that she would leave Sir Philip directly after the ball. He knew that in preparation for this, Mrs. Budge had informed her tenant he must leave at the end of the month. Mr. Davy said that to protect her reputation, Mrs. Budge should return to her own flat for a discreet few months, until their wedding, for he had gone as far as proposing to her.

The earl did not see much of Arabella, although he met her at several functions, for Lady Carruthers was always there and always monopolizing his attention. Furthermore he was ashamed at having kissed Arabella. He was ashamed also of his thoughts when he looked at her, for that half-naked Arabella appeared to be burnt into his brain. How young and virginal she seemed set against his increasingly wicked thoughts. And yet his eyes followed her around the room and he could not bring himself to pay much attention to the other young misses and their mothers who were clamouring for his attention.

It came as almost a relief when Lady Fortescue invited him to the "staff" sitting-room one evening for a consultation about the final arrangements for the ball. Arabella, too, was invited. She found herself looking forward to another "family" evening. Neither she nor the earl had had time to visit the hoteliers.

Not wishing to tell her mother she was going, for she knew Lady Carruthers would insist on being present as well, Arabella once more pleaded a headache, saying she could not go to the Humphreys's turtle dinner but adding mendaciously she had overheard someone say the earl would be there.

With relief, she watched her mother sally forth for the evening before changing into one of her new gowns, a confection of pink muslin with little puffed sleeves and three flounces at the hem. The high waist was bound with a broad silk satin sash. Miss Tonks had supplied a long glass from the hotel store and Arabella whirled round in front of it, admiring the way the fine muslin floated out about her body. She often wondered now if Sir Philip's plan had had any effect. The earl showed no signs of courting her. Certainly he danced with her at balls and talked to her at parties, but he was always correct and a trifle distant. But surely in the comfortable atmosphere of the upstairs sitting-room he would relax a little bit and perhaps she might be better able to judge whether he felt anything for her at all.

The earl was not there when she walked in. She sat down next to Miss Tonks, who hurriedly vacated her seat and went to sit next to Sir Philip so that the earl would be able to sit next to Arabella when he arrived. Mr. Davy was not present and Miss Tonks missed him, missed his friendly face and courteous manner. Unfortunately, she voiced these thoughts aloud.

"I have had enough of that mountebank," complained Sir Philip. "Why don't he get back to business, hey? Who's paying for his keep?"

"He is," lied Lady Fortescue. "You have no reason to complain. We are paying for the horrible Mrs. Budge."

The colonel remembered that Mr. Davy was supposed to be the son of a friend and said, "He is a fine man."

"He's in trade," sneered Sir Philip.

"As are we," pointed out Miss Tonks.

"Ah, here is Lord Denby," said Lady Fortescue with an air of relief. "Now we can get down to business. The accounts, Miss Tonks."

The colonel passed round pieces of paper as the earl sat down next to Arabella. They all wrote busily while Lady Fortescue outlined the amount of money that had come in, the money they would have to lay out, and tried to calculate a reasonable sum to send to the army but which would still leave them in profit.

Again the earl was amazed at the grasp of hard business that these hotel owners had.

"We are finally agreed," said Lady Fortescue at last.

"Except for one thing," said Sir Philip. "Why not make this our swan song and go out in glory? We have all worked hard at this venture. If we put the hotel on the market directly after the ball, we could secure a small fortune for it, divide up the proceeds and retire, me with my Mary, and the rest of you where you will."

Lady Fortescue glanced at Miss Tonks's rigid face and said crossly, "I have no intention of selling this hotel. We will buy your share, Sir Philip, and you may go off with your ... your ... Mrs. Budge."

"You'd never manage without me," jeered Sir Philip. "Who got Miss Carruthers here to be taken about by her mother? You couldn't even manage that."

"We would have hit on something," said the earl stiffly, "had you not volunteered."

"I would not have volunteered had you, sir, not flatly refused to help," pointed out Sir Philip.

"Mind your manners," said the earl coldly.

"Only pointing out the truth," said Sir Philip gleefully—gleeful now that he had everyone riled up.

"Why do you always spoil everything?" demanded Miss

Tonks almost tearfully. "Oh, that Mr. Davy were here. *He* is always a gentleman."

"You silly, lanky spinster, are you saying I am not a gentleman?"

Miss Tonks looked down her long thin nose at him. "That is exactly what I am saying."

"You can hardly call yourself a lady," said Sir Philip, the top of his shining scalp turning puce with anger. "Whoever heard of a lady emptying the slops?"

"It is not what we *do*," countered Miss Tonks, "but what we *are*, and you, sir, are an evil, messy old man through to the bone."

Sir Philip stood up. "I'm going to get drunk," he shouted. "A bottle is better company than you lot any day."

No one tried to stop him from leaving, which put him in an even greater fury.

There was an uncomfortable silence after he had left.

Arabella wished with all her heart that the old, informal atmosphere would return. The colonel said slowly, "Mind you, Sir Philip has a point. There is no need for us to continue with the hotel." He took Lady Fortescue's hand in his. "We could be married and retire to the country."

Lady Fortescue gently disengaged her hand. "We will see."

Arabella saw the look of hurt in the colonel's eyes and thought with wonder, Why, he is in love with her.

The earl, as if recollecting his social manners with an effort, turned to Arabella and asked her whether she had enjoyed a certain breakfast they had both attended, but as Arabella talked, she realized he did not appear to be listening to her, and felt it was all quite hopeless. And the earl, who had been watching the movement of those lips which he had kissed and the rise and fall of that excellent bosom and wondering what it would feel like under his hands was startled to be asked directly, "Do you not agree?"

"Yes, of course, Miss Carruthers," he said quickly.

She looked at him with hurt and contempt. "I just asked you if you did not think it disgraceful that Queen Charlotte should paint herself pink and jump in the pond in front of Buckingham House." She rose to her feet. "You were not listening to a word. I am sorry to have bored you."

Miss Tonks followed her out of the room. "Now, Arabella," she asked as they entered Lady Carruthers's apartment together, "why are you so angry with Lord Denby?"

"He did not even make a pretence of hearing what I said. I am just a silly little miss to him still and I went through all that humiliation at Sir Philip's hands for nothing."

"You never did tell me what Sir Philip arranged."

And so, after swearing her to secrecy, Arabella told her. Miss Tonks raised one thin hand to her flat bosom and said weakly, "But I do not understand! I do not understand *at all*. Why should Sir Philip wish you to appear like a tart?"

"To stop Lord Denby from thinking of me as a school miss."

"I am sure it had that effect, Arabella, but I was so sure, watching you both this evening, that he was listening to you intently. His eyes were firmly fixed on you."

"Oh, I sometimes firmly fix my eyes on Mama when she is giving me a jaw-me-dead and think of something else. All that this ball has caused is a great deal of expense and misery and no one is going to be happy or speaking to each other at the end of it. Mark my words, Letitia."

***

It seemed as if frayed tempers could not get worse, but they did. The hotel was in a constant uproar as decorators draped the downstairs walls with silk and gardeners carried in hothouse plants and guests moodily picked at the worst food they had ever had in the hotel as the temperamental Despard slaved over rehearsals for the menu for the ball supper.

Miss Tonks began to fantasize about murdering Mrs. Mary Budge. Instead of keeping to the fastness of her room and stuffing her face as she had done before, Mrs. Budge began to take a proprietorial interest in the ball and was to be seen lumbering everywhere and attempting to give directions to the workmen. The colonel took Sir Philip aside and told him roundly that if his lady's presence stayed too much in evidence, then certain of their guests might cancel. "And you know why," pointed out the colonel, "or are you totally blinded by love?"

"Mind your own business," snarled Sir Philip. But he saw the force of the colonel's remarks when he found Mrs. Budge talking to Lady Porchester and explaining how she, Mrs. Budge, was going to make the ball a success. Lady Porchester's face was a frozen mask of hauteur, perhaps a little due to the fact that Mrs. Budge was pointing out various flower displays with a half-eaten chicken drumstick which she was holding in one hand.

Sir Philip rushed her off into the office. "Look, sweetheart," he said, "you don't run this here place. You've got an invitation. I'll take that away if you don't keep clear."

"You said I was to be a partner," complained Mrs. Budge.

"Partners in this hotel put in work and money. Miss Tonks has embroidered the initials of each guest on the napkins to be used at the supper table, and Miss Carruthers was not too high in the instep to help her, either. Colonel Sandhurst has been running between the kitchens and the markets trying to find the freshest of produce. We're all doing our bit. Now, is it too much to ask you to behave yourself?"

"You don't love me," said Mrs. Budge sulkily.

"Keep out of the road," said Sir Philip in a flat tone of voice she had never heard him use before, "or I'll take that invitation of yours and tear it up."

Later that day, he saw Mrs. Budge driving off with Mr. Davy but he told himself he was too busy to care.

***

The earl found his thoughts were turning more and more to Arabella. He had been to a ball the night before and she had not been there. He found he had immediately lost interest in the affair. In order to find out what had happened to her, he had taken Lady Carruthers up for a dance. Too late, he found it was the supper dance and so had to endure her company at table. She told him that Arabella was receiving the final fittings for her ball gown, and she, Lady Carruthers, had decided it would be as well if the girl cut down on social occasions until the ball—as the ball was her official coming-out. "And I believe young Fotheringay plans to offer for her," said Lady Carruthers. The earl looked at her, alarmed. "Surely you can do better for Arabella than that!"

Lady Carruthers appeared startled at the familiar use of her daughter's first name but then decided that the earl probably saw himself as the girl's future father. The fact that his courtesy to her was prompted by an interest in Arabella did not cross her mind. "Well, we will see what happens at the ball," she said complacently, and then began to talk about all the gentlemen who had expressed a wish to dance with her. "Then you must favour me with one," he said with automatic gallantry and did not notice the way her eyes began to glow.

As soon as the supper was over, he made his excuses to his hosts and took himself off to his club where he found

Mr. Sinclair sitting moodily in a corner, drinking steadily.

"What has plunged you into the depths?" asked the earl, sinking into an armchair opposite. "And where did you come by that shiner?"

For Mr. Sinclair had a black eye.

"Tarry," he said glumly. "Had the cheek to call at my home and throw some of the trinkets I had given his wife at my feet."

"I trust, for your sake, that Joan, Mrs. Sinclair, was absent?"

"That's the devil of it. She was there and heard the whole thing."

"Is she still with you?"

"Only because she wants to go to that ball at that damned hotel. After that, she says she is taking herself off to the country and then she will consult her lawyers about divorce proceedings."

"So Tarry blacked your eye?"

"Evidently," said Mr. Sinclair sourly. "I tried to tell Joan that it was simply the fashion to give admired actresses trinkets. Everyone did it, I said.

"She pointed out that Mr. Tarry evidently did not think so. She is threatening to go to the theatre to see him so that he can give evidence in the divorce case. What am I to do?"

The earl looked at him thoughtfully. "Tell me exactly what happened, how he arrived at your house, where your wife was when he arrived, everything."

"I don't see it makes much difference, but ... Oh, well, my butler announced Mr. Tarry. Joan was not in the room. Before I could say I was not at home, Tarry pushed his way in. He began quietly enough, wanted to know what I had been doing with his wife, and so on. I answered that I was guilty of nothing but admiration. He began to become angry. Said his wife's reputation was worth more than gold. I tried to reason with him. He began to shout. Joan heard the noise and came into the room. That was when he pulled the trinkets out of his pockets and threw them on the floor and then he punched me in the eye and left."

"Sheer frustration, my friend," said the earl, beginning to look amused. "What does Tarry look like?"

"Tall, thin fellow, with black hair and a gallows face."

"When I attended that rehearsal," said the earl, "I saw what I now take to be Mr. Tarry standing a little way behind his wife, in the shadows. He saw you presenting that necklace to his wife and did nothing. By the way, was that one of the trinkets he handed back?"

"No, just some little gewgaws I gave her, usually bracelets and things like that."

"What you were supposed to do was to buy him off. He said she was worth more than gold. That was the clue. If you pay him a healthy sum, he will tell your wife anything you wish her to hear."

"Are you sure of this?"

"Why else would he wait so long? Were you on the point of demanding … er … your reward for all these gifts?"

Mr. Sinclair had the grace to blush. "As a matter of fact, I had suggested it."

"So husband and wife got together to try to think up some clumsy scheme to get a good payment out of you. I am sure money will get you out of it."

"I hope you are right. Bye the bye, I gather this grand ball is to bring out that Carruthers chit."

"Miss Carruthers is a friend of mine and a very beautiful lady," said the earl coldly.

"Oho, so that's the way the land lies. Going to steal a march on all the young fellows and take the prize yourself?"

The earl got to his feet. "You are such a vulgar character, Sinclair. No wonder you become embroiled with actors."

He went out and walked through the dark night streets of London, oblivious to dangers from footpads. His brain seemed in a turmoil. Arabella married to someone would mean Arabella lying in someone else's arms. The more he thought about it, the more he realized he could not bear it. And then he stopped short and burst out laughing, startling a passing watchman. All he had to do was to marry her himself. He felt quite dizzy with happiness, as if he had just turned a corner of the street and come face-to-face with love.

***

Arabella was sitting with Miss Tonks the following afternoon working out chalk designs. It was not enough at a grand ball to simply chalk the ballroom floor with ordinary white French chalk. The floor had to be chalked in many colours and the designs had to be as perfect as the design on an Oriental rug.

And so, as Arabella bent her head over the paper, she was unaware that the earl was calling on her mother.

Lady Carruthers was very red, for she had been in her bedroom when he was announced and had slapped on too much rouge.

His dislike for this woman made the earl wish to get his business over with as soon as possible.

After exchanging the necessary courtesies, he began, "You will have gathered that I am far from indifferent, my lady. I wish to announce our engagement at this ball, a fitting occasion, I think."

Lady Carruthers, who did not know he was talking about

Arabella, let out a faint shriek and supported herself by putting one trembling hand on a chair-back.

"My lord," she said faintly. "Oh, my lord."

"I have a mind to keep it a surprise until then," he said. "I trust you agree."

"Yes," she said. "Oh, yes."

"Then, after the ball, we will arrange for my lawyers to meet your lawyers and draw up the necessary settlements. Thank you. You have made me the happiest of men."

He bowed and withdrew. Lady Carruthers sat down suddenly. It was the answer to all her wildest dreams. No, she would not tell anyone, not even Arabella. The minx had taken up too much of Denby's attentions. Let her find out in the most dramatic way possible that her own mother's mature charms had secured the prize.

***

On the day of the ball it seemed at first as if everything would go wrong. The servants, infected by the bad temper of their masters, cursed and swore, tripped over each other, shouted and punched. But all at once, by six in the evening, the rooms were magically ready, the whole of the downstairs of the hotel turned into a glittering ballroom lined with long mirrors, banks of flowers, swaths of silk and tall candelabra.

Miss Tonks and Arabella worked feverishly with their coloured chalks, screaming with dismay when a servant crossed the floor to put some last-minute arrangements to the decorations. Arabella was just putting the finishing touches to the last corner when her mother's footman summoned her, saying she was to go above-stairs and be prepared for the ball.

Lady Carruthers had spared no expense on Arabella. Her

ball gown of white muslin was ornamented with seed pearls and gold thread. A coronet of seed pearls and thin gold wire had been hired to decorate her head after Monsieur André had finished with it. A lady's-maid had been engaged to help her get ready, Lady Carruthers needing the sole services of her own lady's-maid. At last Arabella was ready. She knew, looking in the glass, that she had never looked so well. Monsieur André had *burnished* her hair so that it appeared to glitter in the candle-light as much as the fairy-tale coronet on top of it.

She entered the sitting-room at the same time as her mother. Lady Carruthers was also in white muslin, although her head was bedecked by tall ostrich plumes. She stood for a moment looking at the glory that was her daughter, and instead of being filled with maternal pride she experienced a bitter pang of envy and then reminded herself that Denby was to make that dramatic announcement this evening. She could not keep her secret any longer.

"You must wish me happy, Arabella," she said.

"I do. I wish you every success at the ball, Mama."

Lady Carruthers gave a little trill of laughter. "You do not understand. But of course he swore me to secrecy. My engagement is to be announced tonight."

"To whom?" asked Arabella, her mind quickly ranging over the number of middle-aged men with whom her mother had flirted at balls and parties.

"Denby."

Arabella closed her eyes. The pain was almost too great to bear.

There was a scratching at the door. "Lady Fortescue," announced the footman after opening it.

Lady Fortescue's black eyes flew from Arabella's stricken face to her mother's triumphant one and she wondered furiously what Lady Carruthers had been up to.

But she said, "It is time to welcome your guests, Miss Carruthers."

"We are ready," said Lady Carruthers.

"As we are bringing your daughter out, so *we* will be with her on the reception line, not you, Lady Carruthers. Come, child, you look very beautiful although a trifle pale."

Lady Carruthers shrugged but did not protest. Her own moment of glory would soon come.

Arabella stiffened when she reached the hall but she pinned a brave smile on her face and marched up to the Earl of Denby. She curtsied low. "Congratulations," she said. He gave her a puzzled look. He opened his mouth to ask her whether she was being sarcastic or not, but Lady Fortescue snapped, "Here come the first of our guests. Head of the line, Lord Denby. Miss Carruthers, take your place next to him."

And so began all the curtsying and bowing while the earl flashed anxious little slanting glances at the frozen beauty next to him and cursed himself for his own clumsiness and arrogance. Why had he assumed she would have him? She did not look at all happy. If only he could have a word with her in private.

By the time the Prince Regent arrived and the colonel, Lady Fortescue, Sir Philip, and Miss Tonks swelled with pride, Arabella barely noticed the royal personage and the earl was only glad that this fat prince had finally put in an appearance so that he might get a moment alone with Arabella.

The prince walked down the double line of waiting guests, nodding and chatting and joking. Behind him walked his friends, who varied from the fop to the Corinthian, and after them the poor relations with the earl and Arabella. The earl expected that the prince would take Arabella to the floor for the first dance but he had forgotten about the Prince Regent's penchant for elderly ladies. And so it was

Lady Fortescue who was led to the floor, Lady Fortescue who glanced around in a dazed way, hardly unable to believe her own triumph. Sir Philip looked at Lady Fortescue with open admiration in his eyes and said, "What a woman!"

"What? That old stick of a creature?" said a coarse voice at his elbow and he turned and looked at Mrs. Budge, and for the first time since he met her, he heartily wished her at the devil. She was wearing an old-fashioned hooped gown embellished with red-and-white-striped ribbons. She looked a fright.

The earl meanwhile had moved quickly. He took Arabella firmly by the arm and hustled her off into the supper room, which was in a former morning-room adjoining the coffee room. But servants were working laying out food and glasses under the eye of Despard. "Where does that door at the end lead?" demanded the earl.

"The back stairs," said Despard, thinking he never would understand the English, as the earl pushed Arabella towards the door.

"Upstairs," commanded the earl. "If I am not private with you, I will scream."

Arabella, listless and tired, went ahead of him. "Now," he said, stopping on a dark little landing, "what did that sour little 'Congratulations' mean?"

"I was congratulating you on your engagement to Mama," said Arabella in a little voice.

"Has everyone run mad? It is *your* hand in marriage I asked her for."

She looked up at him in a dazed way. And then she said in a wondering voice, "Cannot you do *anything* right?"

He took her in his arms. Her brain was in a turmoil. She opened her mouth to berate him, to demand to know why he had not asked *her*. But before she could speak, he kissed her passionately, and suddenly all the hurt and fright melted inside her. She could feel her whole body *yearning* against his and then everything seemed to whirl about her and she clutched his shoulders for support.

"Why didn't you say anything?" she asked when she could.

"I realized at last how very much I loved you, how I do love you," he said huskily. "Oh, I never dreamt for a moment that mother of yours would think I meant her. And I am to announce our engagement this evening. Well, I am going to do it. Lady Carruthers needs to be punished for all the pain she has given you. Will you marry me?"

She smiled up into his eyes. "Perhaps."

"Oh, Arabella, my sweetheart." He kissed her again while downstairs the dancers performed the Sir Roger de Coverley, their feet thumping on the floor, scattering Miss Tonks's and Arabella's magnificent chalk carpet, their steps acting as a sort of counterpoint to the thudding of the two hearts on the back stairs, pressed so very close together.

* * *

Mr. Davy was dancing with Miss Tonks and Miss Tonks was in seventh heaven, for Mr. Davy was such a beautiful dancer that it seemed to her that her own steps had never been better.

Sir Philip, lounging beside a tub of roses, watched them sourly.

"Where's Denby?" said a voice at his ear.

Sir Philip looked up and recognized Mr. Sinclair, whom he had met many times during drinking sessions at Limmer's. "Somewhere around," said Sir Philip.

"I would like to thank him. Very knowing chap, Denby. Saved my marriage. I'm going to keep clear of actors from now on. What's that creature doing here? Going to entertain us later, hey?"

He pointed with his quizzing-glass to where Mr. Davy was dancing with Miss Tonks.

"Do you mean my Miss Tonks?" demanded Sir Philip wrathfully. "Any more remarks like that and I'll have you thrown out."

"No, no, Davy. Jason Davy. Haven't seen him act in some time but remember him well."

"But that Mr. Davy is a merchant—son of a friend of Colonel Sandhurst!"

"Someone's been bamming you, Sommerville. When did you ever see a Cit dance like that?"

He moved away and Sir Philip sat with his brain churning. So they *had* hired an actor to lure Mrs. Budge away. But there was that Mr. Davy in the City. Must be another Davy. He, Sir Philip, had been tricked by his partners. They would pay for this, and pay dearly.

"There you are, my chuck," cried Mrs. Budge, sailing down on him like some particularly massive bird of prey. "Isn't the supper to be served? Can't we just have a little peek?"

"Not yet," said Sir Philip. She had broken veins on her cheeks. Why had he not noticed that before? "The old morning-room's so small that we can only hope they all don't descend on it at once."

"Aren't we going to sit down to a proper meal?" she asked.

"No, it's stand, take a fork and plate and eat in a crush."

Sir Philip noticed that the earl and Arabella had reappeared. He saw the earl lead Arabella up to the Prince Regent and say something, he saw the prince smile indulgently, and then, when the music ended, he saw the earl hold up his arms for silence.

Lady Carruthers moved forward, her eyes darting this way and that in triumph.

Holding Arabella's hand, the earl said in a loud voice, "I am the happiest of men. Miss Arabella Carruthers has agreed to become my wife."

There was laughing and cheering and then a terrible scream rent the air. Feathered head-dress askew, Lady Carruthers thrust her way forward to the front.

"You're marrying me!" she shouted. "Me, me, ME!"

The earl put his arm about Arabella's shoulders and shook his head.

Lady Carruthers fell to the floor and began to scream and drum her feet in a paroxysm of rage.

Lady Fortescue clasped her thin beringed hands and her eyes shone with delight. The crowning triumph of the evening, a really awful scandal! Society would talk about it for weeks and weeks.

CHAPTER EIGHT

A little work, a little play
To keep us going—and so, good-day!

A little warmth, a little light
Of love bestowing—and so, good-night!
—GEORGE DU MAURIER

For all except Arabella and her earl, a great cloud of anti-climax settled on the Poor Relation. They all felt jaded and tired.

Miss Tonks succumbed to a bad cold and Sir Philip took over the account books, raising spirits a little by saying that even after their donation to the army, they were well in profit.

Mrs. Budge announced she was leaving him. Sir Philip was still smarting at the trick played on him by the others, for he had firmly established that Mr. Davy was indeed an actor; but on the other hand, he did not want to tell Mrs. Budge about the deception, for he was heartily sick of her now and was glad to get rid of her. He was also suddenly tired of hotel life. With the large profit they had made from the ball and with the sale of the business, they could all retire comfortably.

He broached this matter when they were all in the sitting-room, even Miss Tonks, sniffing into a damp handkerchief and decidedly red about the nose.

But Lady Fortescue, although very tired, was still flushed
with success. In her dreams at night she still circled that
ballroom with the Prince Regent, with everyone watching.

"Seems like as good a time as any to sell up," said the
colonel, ever hopeful. "What do you say, Amelia?"

Lady Fortescue looked at his upright figure and for a
moment her black eyes softened, but then she said, "May I
see the books, Sir Philip?"

Sir Philip handed them over. Lady Fortescue bent over
them for a long time, and then said, "Do you know, after
our success, I suggest we raise our prices again, and after
another Season, why, we could all retire and live very well
indeed. In fact, we could all live in the style to which none
of us has been accustomed for many years, or, in your case,
Miss Tonks, has never been accustomed to at all."

"What will become of me?" asked Miss Tonks pathet-
ically. "You, Lady Fortescue, will go off with Colonel
Sandhurst; I do not know what Sir Philip will do, but I will
be left to live alone again."

Sir Philip was feeling exhausted. He had put forward a
sensible suggestion and he had been looking forward to a
life of leisure. His temper broke and he forgot his desire to
be quit of Mrs. Budge.

"While we're on the subject of money," he said nastily,
"how did you fix the books to cover up what you were
paying that mountebank of an actor?"

Miss Tonks looked like a frightened rabbit. "You *knew*,"
she whispered.

"I found out at the ball," said Sir Philip. "She's packing
now, but wait until she hears what I have to tell her. All that
expense for nothing."

"That's blown it," said the colonel when Sir Philip had
marched out.

"The fault was not Mr. Davy's," pleaded Miss Tonks in a tremulous voice. "He played his part well."

"Yes," agreed the colonel. "It is a pity he was found out. But pay him we must. We should have known Sir Philip would not be gulled for long. But it nearly worked."

* * *

Mrs. Budge looked up from a large trunk as Sir Philip entered the room and stood surveying her with an evil grin on his face.

"You can't talk me out of it," said Mrs. Budge. "I'm leaving you for a better man, a younger man, a richer man."

"Like play-actors, do you?"

Mrs. Budge turned and looked at him, holding a large petticoat which she had just folded to her massive bosom. "What you talking about, then?"

"Davy, Mr. Jason Davy, penniless actor, paid by my faithless friends to gull you and lure you away from me. Ah, well, they've succeeded, and they're all next door having a good laugh at you."

"Is this true?"

"Every bit of it. I'll go and get him."

Sir Philip returned shortly with Mr. Davy.

"What is this?" cried Mrs. Budge. "Sir Philip tells me you ain't nothing but an actor in the pay of them next door to trick me into leaving."

Mr. Davy looked at the malicious glint in Sir Philip's eyes and knew the game was up. He spread his hands. "I am afraid that is the case."

"Get out of here," wailed Mrs. Budge. She threw her bulk into Sir Philip's elderly arms. "Oh, my sweetheart, my precious darling, can you ever forgive me?"

Lust stirred in Sir Philip's ancient body. Oh, well, he thought, just one more time.

Mr. Davy walked sadly next door and up to the sitting-room.

"All that for nothing," he said disconsolately. "Do you know that Sir Philip has discovered the deception?"

The colonel nodded. "You nearly did it. You just nearly pulled it off. We will pay you what we promised."

"I cannot take the money for a failure."

"If a play failed but you had played your part well, you would take the money," said Miss Tonks. "Please accept it."

"I quite agree," said Lady Fortescue. "Make out a cheque for the full amount, Colonel."

"You are very good," said Mr. Davy. "I shall miss you all." He took the cheque and bowed. "I must hope that some theatre manager will find a part for me."

"Lord Denby," cried Miss Tonks. "You need a patron. He can help. I will go and see if I can find him."

The earl was in his apartment and listened gravely to Miss Tonks's eager request. "I will see what I can do," he said. "Arabella suggested before that I should be his patron. In fact, I think I know of a way I can do it. I shall call on you this evening and let you know if I have any success."

Delighted, and pink about the nose with a cold in the head and pleasure in the soul, Miss Tonks darted back up the stairs to tell Mr. Davy the glad news.

"So what has happened to Sir Philip and Mrs. Budge?" asked Lady Fortescue after the actor had thanked Miss Tonks.

"They are very much together again."

"I do not want to be driven into selling this place just to get rid of that woman," said Lady Fortescue. "We must think of something else, Colonel."

***

The earl made his way to the theatre, where *The Way of the World* was about to open. He was fortunate in finding Mrs. Tarry in the Green Room. He said he was smitten by her charms. "That is a tawdry necklace you are wearing," he said, raising his voice a little as his eye caught sight of Mr. Tarry standing in the shadows, listening. "You should always wear diamonds. I saw your rehearsal of the play. Such a pity the actor who plays Mirabell is not up to your weight. I confess I feel that my friend, my very dear friend, Mr. Jason Davy, would be better in the part. A pity, for had he the part then, I would have an excuse to call and see you."

The mention of that diamond necklace was still causing her eyes to shine. He kissed her hand and gracefully took his leave, feeling pretty sure of what her next move would be. She would throw a scene and demand that Mr. Davy had the part of Mirabell and that unless Mr. Davy were in the part, she would not go on. All that Mr. Davy had to do was make sure he had a written contract so that the Tarrys would not try to ruin things for him when they found that neither the earl nor any diamond necklace was going to put in an appearance. He felt sure that Mr. Tarry encouraged men to court his wife and give her presents so that the pair could use a genteel form of blackmail.

So he went to Rundell & Bridge and bought a fine diamond necklace, but for Arabella, and was almost sorry for Lady Carruthers when he caught the look of almost blind envy on her face when he clasped the jewels around Arabella's neck later that day.

***

The earl and Arabella visited the sitting-room together that evening and a gratified Mr. Davy learned that he probably had a part and the earl suggested he call at the theatre as soon as possible. The colonel said he would send Mr. Davy's belongings to his lodgings, including his new clothes, and so Mr. Davy decided he would walk immediately to the theatre. Sir Philip was not present and so there was no one to jeer at Miss Tonks when she said quietly that she would see Mr. Davy to the door of the hotel.

They stood together in the hall under the glittering light of the chandelier. Mr. Davy raised Miss Tonks's hand to his lips. "I shall miss you," he said quietly.

"Come back and see us," urged Miss Tonks. "I ... I shall miss you as well."

He bowed and kissed her hand, put his curly brimmed beaver at a jaunty angle on his head and left the hotel.

Miss Tonks hesitated. Then she ran quickly into the street. He was walking away. She could see him clearly in the lights from the shops, his slim elegant figure moving away from her. She stayed where she was, straining her eyes, looking all the way down Bond Street until he turned into Oxford Street, and then he was gone.

***

When she returned to the sitting-room, Sir Philip had joined the party. Despite the fact that Arabella was playing the piano and that everyone else seemed in good spirits, Sir Philip looked sour.

He neither listened to the conversation or the music. He wanted rid of Mary Budge, who now disgusted him after his recent brief and lustful lapse. He also wanted to walk away from the hotel and all its dreary responsibilities, from complaining guests to the Gallic tantrums of Despard, the chef.

"The money from the ball has not yet been lodged in the bank," he realized Lady Fortescue was saying to him.

"I'll take it round in the morning to Coutt's." Sir Philip creaked to his feet. "Going out," he muttered.

He went along to Limmer's. All the talk was of the horse race to take place at Ascot in two days' time. The tables in the coffee room were littered with racing periodicals—*Bailey's Racing Register*, *Pick's Racing Calendar* and *The Sporting Magazine*. Names of horses were being bandied about, and very peculiar some of the names were: Kiss in a Corner, Jack, Come Tickle Me, I Am Little, Pity My Condition, Why Do You Slight Me? Britons Strike Home and Turn About Tommy.

A shadow loomed over Sir Philip as he sat at a table, and there was Mr. Fotheringay. "You should have warned me about Denby," he said. "Snatched the beauty away from all of us."

"Don't talk to me about women," snarled Sir Philip. "I'm sick of women. Horses are more interesting."

Mr. Fotheringay slid into the seat beside him and lowered his voice. "I'll tell you who's going to win at Ascot."

"Everyone always knows who's going to win," said Sir Philip wearily, "and they're always wrong."

"But this is a sure thing. Do you know who owns Lady in Her Petticoat?"

"No. Don't care."

"Lord Black."

"That villain!"

"Exactly. And he's fixed it so that his horse will win."

"How so?"

"I've pulled my horse out of the race, for my jockey says that Black's men are threatening to break the legs of any jockey who rides before his horse."

"Report him to the authorities."

"He's too powerful. Anyway, why don't we make a killing on the race instead? Why should we turn puritan?"

"You're sure of this?"

"Ask Peters. Hey, Peters!"

A Corinthian lounged up. "Bend your head down here, Peters, till we whisper. Ain't it true that Black's fixed the race so as his mount will win?"

"That's what they're saying," said Peters with a grin. "Tell you what, I'm laying a monkey on Lady in Her Petticoat."

Sir Philip ordered wine, then Mr. Fotheringay ordered wine, then Mr. Peters ordered more wine, and the more foxed he became, the more Sir Philip felt his friends and colleagues had used him shamefully. Then, with the sudden seeming clarity of the very drunk, he found the answer to his problems. He would take that money from the ball and put it on this horse of Lord Black's. He would make a killing and return in triumph to the hotel. No longer could Lady Fortescue say she had to hold on for another Season.

Had Sir Philip returned to the hotel to sleep it off, then he might have seen the folly of his ways, but he returned only to pack a bag, collect the money from the safe, and then to journey with a drunken crowd through the night to Ascot. Booked in at a local inn, the roistering continued right up until the race, when Sir Philip, who had never sobered up, was convinced that fortune was staring him in the face.

In fact, when Happy Hunter romped home, the clear leader, and Lady in Her Petticoat was trailing the field, he could not quite believe it. But reality finally struck him and all at once he was stone-cold sober and the money from that ball had melted like fairy gold. Some little grain of common sense had stopped him from putting it all on and he had kept back half. How could he face the others?

It was a sad journey back to Town as they all mourned their losses and vowed never to listen to gossip again.

Sir Philip went straight to the bank and lodged the rest of the money. There was no way he could cover up the loss. Lady Fortescue and the colonel were always calling on the bank manager.

Numb with shame, he trudged into the hotel and sent Jack, the footman, to summon the others.

When they all entered the office, they knew immediately something was up. They had never seen Sir Philip look so cast down before. In a halting voice they had never heard him use before, they heard him tell the tale of how he had lost the money.

There was a long silence when he had finished. The colonel saw all his dreams of living quietly in the country with Lady Fortescue whirl about his head and disappear. Lady Fortescue suddenly felt very old and ill. It was one thing to gallantly say they should go on when there was a comfortable sum in the bank, another to face up to the fact that they were forced to continue to work. Only Miss Tonks was relieved. Miss Tonks decided she was quite prepared to go on forever in this hotel rather than go back to her previous life of loneliness.

Lady Fortescue found her voice. "You must appreciate, Sir Philip, that we cannot trust you to handle any money again. We will pay you a strict allowance and that will need to suffice. It will be less than the rest of us draw in order to make up some of the loss. I trust you agree."

And Sir Philip sadly bowed his head.

The colonel cleared his throat. "You have behaved disgracefully, sir, quite disgracefully. But since we must go on, we must go on in as pleasant a manner as possible. I suggest we put this behind us."

Sir Philip's eyes filled with grateful tears.

And then the office door opened and Mrs. Budge came in.

"What's going on here?" she demanded. "And where have you been, Philip?"

"Mind your own business," snapped Miss Tonks, colouring up.

"Don't get cheeky with me, you old fright," sneered Mrs. Budge.

"That's it," said Sir Philip. "Don't you dare insult my Miss Tonks, not now, not ever. Go and pack your bags, woman, and get out of my sight."

"But sweetheart, light of my life—"

"Get out," screamed Sir Philip, waving his little arms. "Never let me see you again!"

And that, as Lady Fortescue was to say afterwards, was when Sir Philip began to redeem himself.

***

The wedding of Miss Arabella Carruthers to the Earl of Denby took place in London the following spring. The hoteliers were all there in their finery and Miss Tonks was maid of honour, very grand in lilac silk.

Lady Fortescue was worried about Arabella. For although the girl looked beautiful in white satin and Brussels lace, her eyes were sad and the earl looked grim.

The fact was that the unhappy pair had had just about as much of Lady Carruthers as they could stand. After Arabella had left the hotel to return to the country with her mother to prepare for the wedding, she had not seen her fiancé alone. Also, her mother had enlivened the dark months of winter by undermining her confidence, telling her that she would probably be a sad disappointment to an experienced man like the earl.

After the wedding was the breakfast at the earl's town house, presided over by *his* formidable mother, the dowager countess, who had told Arabella that the earl's late wife had been a saint and hinted that no one could ever match up to her. Worse than that, the couple were to spend their honeymoon at the earl's town house, where his mother and Lady Carruthers would be in residence.

So while Arabella's self-esteem was being undermined by her mother, so the earl's love for Arabella was being chipped away by *his* mother, who kept warning him that the girl looked too young and was too flighty.

The wedding service was enlivened for the guests by Lady Carruthers's loud whispers that the earl had really meant to marry *her* before her own daughter, mark you, had lured him away.

With solemn faces the earl and Arabella walked down the aisle of St. George's, Hanover Square, and out into the windy street under the tumbling sound of the bells.

They climbed into the gaily bedecked wedding carriage, which was to drive them to the reception. "I'm going to do something about this," said the earl.

"What?" asked Arabella nervously.

"You'll see," he said moodily.

Sir Philip was travelling in a carriage in the wedding procession with Miss Tonks. He took her hand and smiled at her, baring his best set of china teeth.

"Well, it's you and me again," he said.

Miss Tonks looked sadly out of the carriage window. A torn playbill advertising Mr. Jason Davy in the role of Mirabell fluttered in the wind. She gently drew her hand away.

The wedding breakfast appeared a merry one, apart from the bride and groom. Then, when it was over, the earl approached the colonel and Lady Fortescue and whispered urgently. Then he returned to Arabella and said, "Go above-stairs and change out of that gown and into your carriage dress." His eyes were sparkling and he was smiling for the first time.

"Why?" asked Arabella.

"You'll see. Just do it."

Arabella went up to the large bedroom which she was supposed to share that night with her husband. She ordered the waiting maid to fetch one of her carriage dresses and then, unable to wait to be dressed, scrambled into it herself.

The earl was waiting for her in the hall. He seized her hand and led her outside to where his curricle was waiting.

"Where are we going?" asked Arabella as he picked up the reins and drove off.

"Surprise, my darling."

And Arabella *was* surprised when the carriage stopped at the door of the Poor Relation in Bond Street and there stood Lady Fortescue, Sir Philip, Colonel Sandhurst and Miss Tonks in their wedding finery, waiting to welcome them.

"This is where we will spend our wedding night," said the earl. "The hotel is closed for the month, and we will be the only guests."

Arabella began to laugh with relief. "It's like coming home."

***

The hoteliers went out for dinner that night, not one of them being vulgar enough to say that they did not want to stay in the hotel while the earl and his wife were spending their first evening alone. They had chosen a modest chop-house where the food was good but unpretentious. They sat and chatted easily like the old friends they were, laughing as they imagined the consternation felt by both the earl's mother and Arabella's mother when those formidable ladies found their victims had escaped them.

"How wonderful it is to be waited on," sighed Lady Fortescue, and they all agreed, just as if they did not have John and Betty to wait on them back at the hotel. "We are fully booked for the whole Season despite the horrendous amount of money we are charging."

"We are all the crack," said Sir Philip. "They no longer stay with us to economize on the price of a town house and I believe the matchmaking mamas think they have only to check their plainest daughter in with us to get her married off."

"I miss that actor, Davy," said the colonel, ignoring Sir Philip's sudden scowl. "Friendly fellow. Always good for a laugh."

"Then I have a surprise for you," said Lady Fortescue. "I have purchased tickets for the play. We will all go to see him this very evening."

"Oh, rapture!" cried Miss Tonks, clasping her hands.

"Oh, be still, my heart," sneered Sir Philip.

But nothing could damp Miss Tonks's pleasure for the rest of that evening. With shining eyes, she watched Mr. Davy performing Mirabell, thinking with wonder that she actually knew this god, had talked to him, and that he had said he would miss her.

Only Sir Philip grumbled after the play when Lady Fortescue proposed they go backstage. So once more Miss Tonks stood in the Green Room, once more Mr. Davy kissed her hand, and she treasured every look and every gesture.

***

As Miss Tonks indulged in celibate love, the earl and Arabella tumbled about the great double bed in the hotel's finest apartment, exploring each other's bodies, until Arabella said in a wondering voice, "I never thought I could ever behave in such a shameless way."

"You were shameless enough going to the Pantheon in that dreadful costume."

Arabella had a longing to tell him that it had been Sir Philip's idea all along, but she had given Sir Philip her word and could not break it even now.

"How long do we stay here?" she asked.

"A few days, and then we will go to Italy. And then, after a long time, we will come back and tell Lady Carruthers that there is no way she is going to live with us."

"Mama expects it!"

"Mama can go back to concentrating on getting married herself and leaving us alone." He gathered her to him, pulling her close against his naked body. "Kiss me again, Arabella. I can never have enough of you."

And so the engrossed couple did not hear the quiet footsteps of the poor relations as they made their way up to their sitting-room.

* * *

"Play us a tune, Sir Philip," ordered Lady Fortescue.

"I will play something for Miss Tonks," he said, "for I have never seen her look better."

He smiled at Miss Tonks affectionately and then flipped up his coat-tails and sat down at the piano and began to play.

But Lady Fortescue, noticing that Miss Tonks's eyes were full of happy dreams, knew what had caused that rare illusion of beauty to lighten the spinster's usually plain face.

Miss Tonks was in love.

And not with Sir Philip Sommerville!